"What's going on?" Slocum asked. "You kill this owlhoot with my own gun, then you rob me."

"Is this such a blow to your vanity?" she asked. "You wonder how anyone can make love to you and then do such a thing?"

"Something like that," he said, playing for time. If he kept Juliana talking long enough she'd make a mistake.

"You are a remarkable man, John. It is too bad we did not meet under better circumstances. You will climb back into the bed. Now!"

He obeyed. Juliana retrieved his Colt, wrapped it in his clothing, and tucked the bundle under her arm.

"Do not attempt to follow me. Please believe me when I say I mean you no harm. But I will kill you if you become involved in matters that do not concern you. Goodbye, my love. You *were* good." Juliana flashed him a dazzling smile, then slipped out the door.

Slocum sat on the bed, his anger mounting. No one pushed John Slocum around. Not like this . . .

OTHER BOOKS BY JAKE LOGAN

JAKE LOGAN

SLOCUM'S WINNING HAND

Ⓑ
®

BERKLEY BOOKS, NEW YORK

SLOCUM'S WINNING HAND

A Berkley Book/published by arrangement with
the author

PRINTING HISTORY
Berkley edition/October 1984

ISBN: 0-425-07494-3

A BERKLEY BOOK ® TM 757,375
Berkley Books are published by The Berkley Publishing Group,
200 Madison Avenue, New York, N.Y. 10016.
The name "BERKLEY" and the stylized "B" with design are trademarks
belonging to Berkley Publishing Corporation.

PRINTED IN THE UNITED STATES OF AMERICA

1

"You like singing girl, velly much, cheap," came the heavily accented pitch. John Slocum stepped past the Chinese pimp hawking his whores and tried to ignore the man. He tugged at Slocum's sleeve. "Two bit feelie, four bit—"

"Not interested," said Slocum. And the Chinaman was no longer interested in him, either. A sailor came staggering down the crowded San Francisco street, an empty bottle in one hand and his other waving a battered cap about in a vain attempt to keep his balance.

Slocum watched as the Chinaman went over and "helped" the sailor. In a few minutes, if the merchant marine had any money left from his drinking binge, it would be gone—safely tucked away in the Chinaman's voluminous sleeves—and the sailor would never know what happened.

Slocum snorted and shook his head. At least, if the man were shanghaied and sold onto a steamer going to the Orient, he'd already know the ropes. That might have been how he became a seaman in the first place. Slocum didn't know or much care. He judged the weight of a few gold double eagles in his pocket and was feeling lucky with them.

Luck. That was something the tall, midnight-haired man hadn't seen much of recently. A placer claim in the Sierras had turned out to hold nothing but back-breaking hours of wet, cold work and no gold. The only bright spot had been the claim jumpers.

Slocum smiled to himself and lightly touched the worn grips of his Colt Peacemaker. Four slugs from that .44–40 had removed the threat of the claim jumpers once and for all. And Slocum wasn't about to let the two hundred in gold the bushwhackers had on them go to waste. Dead men didn't need gold for whiskey or much else.

Walking down Jackson Street, Slocum turned and went on past Portsmouth Square and headed for East Street, running parallel along the Bay. The sight of the sailor had told him at least one ship was in port. He knew from experience that the sailors got careless with money that had just been paid out. For months on end they'd been alone and at sea and now their pay burned a hole in their pockets. Slocum saw no reason why he shouldn't be the one to teach the salts something about odds and how to really play poker.

He touched the cuff holster holding his Remington .41 double derringer. Slocum didn't figure on needing it at all, but the San Francisco waterfront was not the sort of place to take a Sunday stroll. On either side of the street were the notorious deadfalls, the saloons and whorehouses that made the Barbary Coast infamous up and down the length of the Pacific coast. Stretching out on several docks were dives even worse. Slocum had patronized most of them at one time or another and found them to be just what he needed. But not now.

He walked into McGuire's Saloon and Bistro and stopped, his green eyes slowly scanning the crowd. Slocum smiled. This was to his liking. Sean McGuire ran a good place, meaning he didn't allow armed robbery inside the walls of his establishment—whether by patrons or his own staff. Anything else went, and usually did.

Slocum went to the long, stained teakwood bar and said, "Got a bottle of Billy Taylor back there?"

"Sure do," the barkeep said, reaching underneath the bar and pulling out a bottle of whiskey that was three-quarters filled. Slocum paid full-bottle price; that was the way it was done. But Sean McGuire prided himself on running an honest saloon: The amber fluid in the bottle was real whiskey. Slocum tasted it and figured it might actually be the brand printed on the label.

"Any good games going?" he asked the barkeep.

"One or two. That one, with the dude and the specials. Might be a few bucks in it for someone with a feel for the cards."

Slocum studied the dude and decided to avoid that game. The man cheated—and poorly—but no one else mentioned it because the "specials" were sitting in. The volunteer policemen probably got a cut from the dude at the end of the evening for keeping the others in the game from protesting too much. This wasn't Slocum's style at all.

"Nothing else?"

"Not unless you speak them Russkies' lingo. A boatload of them steamed into the harbor this morning. Been boozin' it up something fierce. Figure on throwing them out in a bit."

Slocum knew this meant that the sailors' money had about been spent up.

"Can't say I speak Russian, but I got along pretty good with a couple of them up in the Sierra Madres."

"You don't have the look of a miner," the bartender said, eyeing Slocum.

"And how's a miner supposed to look?"

"No offense." The barkeep's eyes dropped to the Colt and didn't lift back to Slocum's eyes. "How about a clean glass?" He shoved the brightly shining shot glass across and took the one Slocum had used. Without another word, he moved on down the bar to serve up tepid beer for a pair of the Russian sailors.

The way their pockets bulged told him that they were still flush.

"Here," Slocum said, "you don't want that stuff. Try this." He poured from his bottle.

"Spaseeba," one said. The other one nudged him in the ribs and he quickly said in heavily accented English, "We thank you. Our English is not so good."

Slocum poured them each another drink, and then they insisted on buying him one. He let them. The wad of greenbacks the one flashed convinced Slocum that his time wasn't wasted and the whiskey had gone to good use. The sailors weren't drunk when he invited them for a small game of poker. Whether they ended up drunk later was their business. Slocum usually played fair, but if the other men didn't show the common sense God gave a goose, that was their lookout.

They found a table in the corner of the room and started a round of stud poker. Three others soon joined them. Slocum had played enough poker to know all the ways of cheating. Sometimes he'd had to use them to get enough money just to survive, but not tonight. Tonight he had found a pair of Russian pigeons who knew nothing about cards and seemed perfectly willing to lose everything for the pleasure of his company—and his willingness to buy the whiskey.

For every dollar he spent on liquor, he won twenty from the sailors.

The others in the game came and went, but Slocum and the two Russians were consistent players, and

Slocum was the consistent winner.

"You been in port long?" Slocum asked.

The one named Stephan answered, his English better than his friend Georgi's.

"Only this morning. We find San Francisco fine place. Lovely foggy place, after so many weeks at sea. We come sailing all way in from Archangel."

Georgi rattled off something in harsh Russian. Stephan waved him off, laughing.

"My friend he says I speak too much. What is difference if you know we come from Archangel rather than Singapore, eh?"

Slocum dealt the hand, bet only a few dollars, and lost to Georgi. The Russian laughed delightedly and slapped him on the back. "My luck turns for gooder. I will, how do you say it, clean you out this night. Then Stephan and I go to find women!"

"Plenty of them around San Francisco," admitted Slocum. "But expensive, if you know what I mean."

"We must win much to buy women," Stephan said solemnly to Georgi. "And we will! Trip was disastrous, but we lived to boast of it. We will again be lucky."

"What happened on the trip?" asked Slocum, his mind on the play. If Stephan wanted to talk, let him. It made his play all the more erratic.

"Storms! Never should we cross North Pacific in December. For a full month we battled waves hundred feet high! The New Year of 1884 was spent fighting bilge pumps." Stephan's voice lowered as he said, "My good friend Sergei was washed overboard on New Year's Day."

"Sorry to hear that."

"But we, Georgi and I, we make it through just fine." Again Georgi rattled off a long string of Russian. Slocum got the feel that the two were hiding something. Whatever secret a Russian sailor had couldn't be of any importance to him. All Slocum cared about—and was accumulating—was the stack of greenbacks on the table. Lady Luck rode on his shoulder this night. Not only did he win from the increasingly drunk Russian sailors, he won from the nearly sober men who occasionally joined in. He had already turned his two hundred dollars into five, each of the Russians contributing about a hundred.

Georgi said something and Stephan suddenly stood and swung. The heavy fist caught the slighter sailor on the side of the head and knocked him to the floor.

"No fighting," said Slocum, his voice low and cold. "Either play or leave."

"Georgi, he say that we should save our money and stay here."

"Plenty of Russian emigrants around," said Slocum. To the north was a large Russian settlement dating back some fifty years or more when the Russians had the idea of colonizing in North America. They had been convinced by Seward to sell Alaska, but they had maintained their small community north of San Francisco until the distance between Mother Russia and the handful of settlers had worn them down. Slocum didn't rightly know if any pure Russians remained around Bodega Bay, but he had run into any number of descendants of the original "colonists," as they called themselves.

"Things are not so good in Russia," Stephan said. Georgi glared up at him from the floor. The fallen sailor made no effort to rise. "Tsar Alexander is a tyrant!"

"Stephan!" cried out Georgi. Stephan ignored him.

Georgi sat up, then got heavily to his feet and left without another word.

"Something about you not liking your tsar bother him?" Slocum asked, curious. Politics left him cold. He had fought a war over politics, states' rights, slavery, and it had brought him nothing but pain. His brother Robert had been killed during Pickett's Charge at Gettysburg. Even after all these years, the memory was still painful. Slocum's hand went to a vest pocket and lightly traced around the watch there—his brother's. He had mailed it home to his parents, only to get it from them years later, after even more pain and heartbreak.

Quantrill. Slocum had ridden with Quantrill and murdered with the best of them, and all because he was a captain in the Confederate army. And he'd been badly wounded because of his complaint about the viciousness of Quantrill's attack at Lawrence, Kansas. He had no good feelings about Quantrill or the politics that caused the war to go on for so long.

Carpetbaggers. A dead judge who had stolen Slocum's farm in Calhoun County, Georgia. A trail sniffed out by lawmen and bounty hunters at various times. No, John Slocum had no love of politics or the men drawn to it. He certainly had no love for a Russian tsar.

"Tsar Alexander is a pig," Stephan declared loudly. Then, like a small child caught with his hand in the cookie jar, he glanced around, his heavy eyebrows working like drunken caterpillars. The dark eyes beneath took on a furtive look that Slocum didn't much care for. "Georgi is right. I should not say such terrible things. You might be . . . one of them."

"Have a drink. And I'm not 'one of them,' whoever

you're talking about. I just enjoy a friendly card game."
Slocum wanted nothing more than to get back to the
business at hand, and for him, this was business. He
figured he was giving the Russian what he wanted.
A good time in exchange for the money. Stephan won
enough small pots to keep him interested but lost the
larger ones through poor play and his drunkenness.

"You boys gettin' tired of playin'?" asked one of
the whores. Slocum looked up and froze her with a
glance.

"Davooska," the sailor said, putting his arm around
the woman's thick waist. "My little precious one."

Slocum fought down a rising tide of anger at the
whore. She was only plying her trade, but she didn't
have to cut in on his trade to do it, though. Stephan
still had plenty of money left from his sea pay. From
all Slocum had been able to gather, Tsar Alexander
might not be well liked—at least by Stephan—but
he paid his sailors enough to get them back aboard
ship.

"Here," Slocum said, handing the woman two bits.
"Go get yourself a drink. My friend is about done
playing. When he's finished I'm sure he'll ask for
you."

The tone he used dismissed the whore. She left,
more than a little frightened by Slocum's expression.

"My darling," the Russian sailor cried out. "Do
not go."

"Are you in or out, Stephan?" asked Slocum. "If
you're out, you just lost all you anted up."

Confused, the Russian stared at the money he'd
already bet, then turned to follow the ass-waggling
whore as she moved along the bar, going from one
man to another.

"How much is she?" Stephan asked.

"More than you have left, but not if you win the pot," said Slocum. He glanced at his cards. Even though all Slocum had were a pair of aces and a pair of treys, he doubted Stephan had anything to beat it. The Russian did not bluff well, and he had been bluffing.

"Then I play out this hand. I call you."

Slocum turned over his cards and waited. Stephan's face melted. All he had was a pair of kings.

"Looks like that about cleans you out," said Slocum, pulling in the money. He tensed now, his hand near the butt of his pistol. The sailor's expression had turned from cheerful to nasty.

"I am wanting my money back to buy a whore."

"You lost. The other gentlemen in the game'll tell you it was honest, too."

"I not saying you cheat. No one cheats Stephan Vladimirov! I want only chance to win back my money."

"How?" asked Slocum. "If you don't have anything to bet, there's no point in me risking all this." He had about six hundred dollars now, two hundred of it his original stake.

Stephan looked around, then bent forward and said in a conspiratorial whisper, "I have something of great value. I put it up against all your money. We play final hand to see who is winner."

Slocum gave a curt nod. He did not believe that the Russian had anything worth six hundred dollars, but if he did, Slocum wanted a look at it. He had already made plans for traveling up the coast, maybe to Oregon. This was a good time to get established in horse dealing. By the time spring came, men needed horses in a bad way to move around. But six hundred dollars wouldn't buy much in the way of animals.

Twelve hundred would. If Stephan's little secret amounted to a hill of beans.

"This," said Stephan, reaching into an inner pocket and pulling out a small, square package wrapped in oiled sealskin. He put it on the table between them. To the others sitting and watching, Stephan said, "This is between us. Go!"

"Please," added Slocum. The other three men shrugged and left to belly up against the bar. Slocum's luck had run too good for them to press it. A chance to get out of the game with only small losses was their best break of the evening.

"It is worth many, many times more than the money you hold. Here. Look. But not to let others see it."

Stephan's words slurred heavily now, and with the ponderous accent Slocum had trouble deciphering what the sailor said. He gingerly took the sealskin pouch, not knowing what to expect. Whatever was wrapped inside was moderately heavy and had raised designs on the sides, and maybe tiny legs.

Slocum unwrapped the package and simply stared.

"It's not like anything I ever saw before," he admitted. The miniature pianoforte was hardly three inches long, but the details were meticulous.

"It is of Siberian jade," Stephan said. "Tsar Alexander accepts nothing less." Slocum ignored the bitter tone and picked up the tiny piano and studied it more closely.

Jade sides were chased with green gold rosettes, lyres, and two mythical creatures Slocum couldn't identify—but he knew the wings on the cat with a woman's head couldn't be from anything found in this or any other world. He opened the hinged top and peered inside. The jade box was empty, but Slocum hardly cared.

"This is real gold?" he asked. The tip of his thumb-nail put a tiny groove in the chasing. Real.

"Beautiful," said Stephan. "We play one more hand. Winner takes it all, as you Americans say?"

Slocum found it hard to force himself to put down the jade pianoforte. He wanted to examine it even more, to get lost in the detail the artisan making it had lavished on his perfect creation.

"All or nothing," he agreed.

Slocum let Stephan deal, watching the man carefully. While he doubted that the Russian was any less drunk than he seemed, Slocum had watched enough unsuspecting men suckered by their own greed. As far as he could tell, Stephan dealt the five-card draw-poker hand fairly.

Slocum's face locked into a mask. He had been getting low cards all night long, and this was no exception. There was a single trey—and four deuces.

"I'm happy with these," he said. Stephan took three.

"And I call you with these," the Russian sailor said, proudly dropping the hand onto the table and showing the three jacks. He reached for the pot but Slocum stopped him, showing the four deuces.

"Sorry, Stephan, but you lose."

For a long instant, the sailor sat as if someone had hit him with a spar. He shook his head, swallowed the last of his whiskey, and then bellowed like a bull.

"*Nyet!* You cannot have it. It was not mine to lose!"

"You should have thought of that before betting," Slocum said. He had expected some trouble, but this irritated him. He hated poor losers. He had gone out of his way to make the Russian feel that the game was fair—it had been—and there was no call for him to raise such a ruckus now. He had lost. And that was that.

Slocum stood, his hand inches from the butt of his Colt. The saloon went quiet, and Slocum had the feel of being on stage, all eyes watching the little drama unfold. He didn't want to shoot the Russian sailor. But he would, if he had to.

"What's getting you boys all riled up?" came a congenial voice. A big, red-nosed Irishman waddled over, his potbelly bouncing as he moved. "I'm Sean McGuire, and this is my place. Either of you got any complaints about that?"

Slocum never took his eyes off Stephan. The sailor backed off, hand inside his dark blue wool tunic.

"If he comes out with a gun, he's a dead man," Slocum said.

"Hell and damnation, he won't do no such thing, will you, bucko?" McGuire turned tiny pig-eyes on the Russian. "No, he won't. Why don't I buy you both a drink, and then you can get along, peaceful-like."

"He has . . . something of mine."

"Stephan lost at cards." Slocum pointed to the hands still face up on the table. McGuire didn't even bother to look. He gestured and two burly men appeared. Each grabbed an elbow and lifted Stephan off his feet and threw him out the back way into the alley. McGuire had no time for losers, only the winners—they had the money.

"The offer stands. You want a drink? On the house, of course. And maybe you'd be a-wantin' a bit more of McGuire's hospitality? There are ladies enough to go around." The huge Irishman slapped Slocum on the back and guided him toward the bar. "Ferddie, a drink for my friend." McGuire slapped Slocum once more and then wandered off, other concerns on his mind.

"You want some company?" asked the whore who had tried to pull Stephan away from the game before Slocum had finished with him.

"Not yours," he said.

"I . . . I'm sorry about that. I shoulda know'd better, but things have been slow. This is the first boat that's docked in over a week. Winter storms keep them out. Some put in to Hawaii and are late arriving. You know how it can be." The woman almost pleaded with Slocum.

"I know how it can be," he agreed. She smiled, showing one broken tooth in front and the rest either yellowed or black. Slocum bought her a drink and thought of sitting in on the other poker game now that the specials and their captive cardsharp had moved on.

Slocum decided it was time to find another place. The six hundred dollars in gold and greenbacks rode heavy in his pocket—but not as heavy as the miniature jade pianoforte. It would take a day or two finding the proper people along Montgomery Street, but he figured to sell it for a princely sum. The wealthy of San Francisco would dearly love something as intricate and well-wrought to sit in their parlors.

"Give it back. I must have it back!" came the slurred words. Slocum didn't have to turn to see who spoke. A quick glance in the mirror behind the bar showed Stephan standing near the back door, a ponderous gun held in unsteady hands. He cocked the single-action revolver and stumbled forward.

When he was ten feet away Slocum turned and looked into the face of death. Stephan's finger tensed on the trigger.

2

Slocum got some idea of what it was like to stare at an oncoming locomotive while trapped in a train tunnel. The bore of the gun Stephan held in shaking hands had the same feel.

"You don't want to shoot anyone, Stephan," Slocum said in a low voice. The last thing in the world he wanted to do was spook the Russian sailor—and if he did scare him, it might be the last thing he ever did. Slocum knew there was no way he could get his Colt out before Stephan jerked off a shot. He was fast, but he wasn't that fast.

No man was.

"Give me box. I must have box back." Sweat beaded on Stephan's forehead, and the alcohol had taken its toll. He wobbled around, his eyes threatening to spin to the top of his head. But the sailor wasn't close enough to passing out to do Slocum any good.

"You lost it in a fair game. You even dealt," Slocum said, more to gain time than to convince the man. Giving the jade miniature back to the Russian wasn't all that much to Slocum's liking, but it sure as hell beat getting a slug pumped into his body.

"Give it to me," Stephan demanded.

"Drink?" asked Slocum, indicating the almost empty bottle of whiskey and a pair of shot glasses on the bar. "No? Mind if I have one? You're making me right nervous waving that gun around."

Slocum turned and poured two drinks with a steady hand. He took a deep breath and kept himself under stern control. To panic now would panic the Russian, and lead would fly in all directions. Many had already left the saloon, but most sat or stood stock-still, paralyzed with the notion of dying from a stray bullet.

"No more drinks. Give it to me!" Stephan's voice ran up the scale and broke in a frenzy of emotion. Tears ran down the man's cheeks. Slocum knocked back one of the glasses and gripped the other one in his left hand.

"You need this, Stephan," he said. "Go on, take it. It's not going to hurt you any."

The instant the Russian's eyes darted to the glass, Slocum acted. The liquor flew out of the glass and into the sailor's face. The glass followed and made Stephan jerk back instinctively. By then Slocum had taken the two steps forward and clamped a powerful left hand around the man's wrist.

Stephan, although drunk, was strong from working at sea for so long. He pulled free of Slocum's grip—but for the Russian this was too late. With his right hand Slocum had drawn his Colt. He brought the heavy gun crashing down onto the side of his assailant's head. The Russian sailor crumpled to the floor, blood gushing from the cut opened by the front sight on Slocum's pistol.

Slocum let Stephan fall unimpeded. He stepped away and wiped the blood off his barrel and the sight and returned the Colt to his holster. The dark-haired man turned to the barkeep and said, "One more. For the road."

"Yes, sir," the barkeep said, his hands moving quickly to obey.

"What in bloody hell's happenin' down there?" came Sean McGuire's bellow. "Can't leave for a second without some jackass causin' me a world of trouble."

McGuire came down the stairs, still buttoning up his fly as he faced Slocum. The whore who had almost lured Georgi and Stephan from the card game trailed McGuire from the cribs upstairs. She tried to smooth her skirts but botched it. Slocum wondered if the woman was any better in bed than she was at getting men there in the first place. Still, he decided, she might not be doing too badly if she and McGuire snuck off now and then.

"No trouble," said Slocum. He downed his whiskey and made a wry face. "Just leaving."

McGuire looked down at the fallen Russian sailor. Stephan stirred and moaned feebly.

"Poor loser, eh? We can take care of him."

Slocum didn't ask how that would be done. It was little concern to him. If Stephan had asked him nice to return the jade box, he probably wouldn't have done it, but now that the sailor had tried to rob him of it, Slocum would be damned before he returned it for less than the six hundred he had risked against it in the card game.

The sailor obviously didn't have that kind of money.

Without another word, Slocum turned and walked out. Even before he reached the door, the saloon's normal noisy hustle and bustle had returned. He had given the patrons a moment of excitement, nothing more. The thrill past, they concentrated again on their drinking and cards and whoring.

Slocum looked up and down the foggy street. He

set off briskly, going east, followed the curving street, cut over a few blocks, then doubled back and waited awhile in the doorway of a dry-goods store.

He didn't think Stephan had trailed him from the saloon. The sailor hadn't even been conscious when he left, but the ruckus had alerted everyone in McGuire's to the fact that Slocum had been a winner and had a sizable roll. The Barbary Coast of San Francisco was no place to advertise more than a bent half eagle—and even the lure of gold in that five-dollar piece might buy a bullet in the back.

Slocum bided his time. He pulled out a Havana and struck a lucifer. The sudden flame made him squint. He lit the tip of the cigar and inhaled with real satisfaction. The tiny glowing orange coal might be visible a few feet away in the fog and give him away, but he figured the odor of the smoke was more likely to reveal him to an astute tracker. Slocum didn't care at the moment. If anything, he wanted anyone on his trail to find him. He was protected here and able to fight his way out of about any scrape.

The blue smoke filtered down in his lungs and relaxed him further. It had been a good night, even considering the run-in with the Russian sailor. He had more than enough money to travel up north to Oregon to find himself a string of those fine, strong Appaloosas and see if he couldn't make a few dollars trading. San Francisco had about run out of interest for him.

Not hearing any sounds in the fog-shrouded street, he puffed out the last of his Havana and started toward his hotel a few blocks west of Portsmouth Square.

Slocum had lived most of his life shooting at men and being shot at. He'd developed a feel for when someone was tracking him. The hair on the back of his neck rose and tickled. Without moving abruptly, he half turned and put his hand on the butt of his Colt.

"Do you have another lucifer? I would appreciate it greatly if you could give me a light." The voice came out of the fog, disconnected from a physical body. And Slocum wanted very much to see who spoke in such cultured, refined tones, whose every word was a sensuous caress and a bold challenge.

With his left hand, he pulled out another lucifer and struck it on a gas lamp post. The surge of light pushed back the enveloping fog and allowed him to see the dark silhouette standing a few feet away. A heavy cloak pulled around feminine shoulders prevented a good look at the body, and the face stayed a mystery in a vagrant swirl of fog.

He held out the sputtering lucifer, silently beckoning the woman to step forward.

A slender hand held out a tiny, tapering, brown-wrapped cigar unlike any Slocum had ever seen. The face stayed hidden as the woman cupped his hand in both of hers and inhaled, lighting the tip of her cigar.

"There is nothing quite like the Egyptian cigarette. Nowhere in the world is finer tobacco grown."

"I'm partial to Cuban. And Virginian broadleaf isn't all that bad, either," Slocum said, intrigued. He caught the potent smoke spiraling from the ridiculously small cigar. It made his head spin. If he'd tried a Havana-sized cigar of this weed it would have knocked him flat on his ass.

"The Havana, such as you smoke, is mild," the woman said. She was obviously taunting him. Rather than irritating him, it made Slocum even more curious.

"Do you walk the streets this late every night?" he asked. "The Barbary Coast isn't much of a place for a lady."

"Who says I am a lady? How do you know I am not one of the whores?" A cloud of smoke hung around the woman's face and mixed with the fog. Slocum still hadn't gotten a good look at her yet.

"A gentleman always believes the best of a woman, on first meeting."

"Unless circumstances prove otherwise," she finished. When she laughed, Slocum thought silver bells rang in the night. It had been a while since Slocum had found a woman like this. She showed more than a little daring even being out alone in the Barbary Coast after dark, she was educated, and she had lingered to talk.

"May I escort you to your destination?" Slocum asked.

"Perhaps that would be a good idea. When the fog rolls in this heavily, I become . . . disoriented."

She glided forward, and her arm smoothly linked with Slocum's. He relaxed and took his right hand away from his Colt. If she had meant him any harm, she could have shot him down using the fog as cover; he didn't doubt she had stood watching him for several minutes as he smoked his Havana.

They had walked about a block when Slocum asked, "Where are we going?"

"Your hotel room must provide a cozy alternative to this cold, wet fog," she said.

"What makes you think I have a hotel room?"

"You are not one of the locals. You do not have that hard edge to you." Her hand lightly brushed over the front of Slocum's trousers, lingered for a moment, then drifted away, as if nothing more than a wisp of fog. "But you do have something hard about you," she said. The soft chuckle made Slocum all the more aware of her effect on him.

"You either guess or you know a lot about me."

"I know nothing but what I see," she said. "I see a handsome man, a gentleman in a city of pimps, thieves, and murderers, a man willing to share an evening with me."

"That's mighty bold of you," Slocum said.

"Do you object?"

She stopped and turned to face him fully. For the first time he got a good look at her. Cascades of wavy ebony-black hair fell away from a gorgeous heart-shaped face painted with perfectly applied cosmetics. Her bright blue eyes were offset by the mascara, and faint pinkish blushes trailed back along high cheek-bones. The nose was straight, beautiful, aristocratic. The lips were a trifle too thin for Slocum's tastes, hinting at cruelty, but this was such a minor quibble he wasn't going to let it get in his way.

She stood tall, only a few inches less than his six foot one, and her appraisal of him was as bold as his of her.

"You are very handsome," she said. Those dark-painted thin lips parted invitingly as her eyes closed. Slocum wasn't going to pass up the opportunity. He kissed her and found passion unleashed. Her finger-nails dug at his back, and she crushed her lips against his as if she couldn't get enough.

The woman broke free, panting, her face naturally flushed now. A tiny pink tongue slipped from between her lips and made a slow circuit before vanishing.

"You are more of a man than any I have had in some time," she said in a husky whisper. "Let us not delay."

"My room's only a few more blocks from here," Slocum said, his feelings matching hers. That single kiss had set his heart pumping hard. He wanted more of what she was so willingly offering.

This time she did not lock arms with him. Her arm circled his waist and kept him close, as if she were afraid he might run off. Slocum's own arm circled her shoulders and held her equally as tight, to let her know that was the last thing on his mind. The dead last thing.

The clerk behind the desk snorted in disgust when he saw Slocum entering with the woman, then the expression changed to one of stark admiration when he saw the woman's beauty. In the well-lit lobby Slocum got a better look at her too, and he definitely approved. She wore the long, dark silk cloak over a dress decorated with soft bits of fur at collar and cuff. The floor-length wine-colored velvet skirt whirled out around her legs, and, as she went up the stairs, Slocum caught sight of slender ankles and trim calves.

He had the door to his room open in a flash. And even faster, the woman spun about and into the circle of his arms for another kiss. This one was no less passionate than the one in the street. Her darting pink tongue slid between her lips and stroked over Slocum's, then parted his lips and found his tongue. The erotic dance of their tongues back and forth mimicked what would be happening lower down in just a few minutes.

But there was no need to rush. This was more excitement than Slocum had counted on finding. The woman responding so in his arms was no whore being paid for her body. She was sensuous, alive, responding because he excited her as much as she did him.

Nimble fingers unfastened Slocum's gunbelt, but he pushed her away when she started to unbutton his shirt.

"I'll do it," he said. The thick roll of money had

been stuffed in one of the shirt pockets, and in the other was the jade box he'd won from the Russian sailor. Slocum discarded the shirt, unfastened the cuff holster holding the .41 derringer, and kicked off his boots. All the while the woman sat on the edge of the bed, watching, saying nothing. But the way her blue eyes danced, Slocum knew she was enjoying the sight of his undressing.

"Keep going," she said. "Do not let me inhibit you."

"Inhibit?" he asked. Then Slocum laughed. He wasn't in the least bit embarrassed to be seen naked in front of a woman. But he wanted her equally as buck naked.

"All in good time," she told him. Again the tongue flashed forth to wet her lips. The sight of her, even fully clothed, made Slocum even harder. He skinned out of his trousers, and his longjohns followed. He stood before her, his organ jerking to the beat of his pulse.

"So huge," she said, reaching out to lightly touch it. "But I expected nothing less from such a man."

The woman dropped to her knees, hands cupping his balls almost reverently. Slocum gasped when she enmouthed him. The sudden warmth surrounding his length, the soft suction applied to the very tip, the way she massaged and soothed, then aroused all made him weak in the knees. He laced his fingers in her lustrous dark hair and guided her up and down in a motion that let him keep control, yet kept him at the very edge.

"So good," she murmured. Without taking her mouth away from his groin, she turned. Slocum got the idea. He began unbuttoning her blouse with the fancy fur at the edges.

"What kind of fur is this?" he asked. He gulped when her mouth gave him a special hot, wet kiss.

"Sable," she said. Every syllable she spoke sent hot winds gusting past his balls. The woman's quick tongue laved at the sides of his shaft, found the bumps and valleys and places most likely to thrill him. And all the while Slocum kept tugging at her blouse.

It fell open to reveal twin mounds of succulent white flesh that bobbed about enticingly. Hard, dark nipples capped the creamy slopes. Slocum took them between thumb and forefinger and rolled them around. It was the woman's turn to moan now.

"You are so good," she sobbed out. "I cannot wait longer. I need you now. One moment!" She stepped out of her skirt. She wore nothing under it. The woman was gloriously exposed for his personal enjoyment now. Slocum sucked in his breath and held it. Long, slender legs moved chastely to hide the shadowy triangle between her thighs. She reached out to him.

Slocum lay back on the bed and she dropped heavily on top. He absorbed the shock of her landing and rolled over, pinning her beneath. Wanton thighs parted, and the dark-furred triangle opened invitingly for him. She eagerly reached down and gripped his length, tugging him insistently forward.

"Hurry, now. I need you inside me. Hurry!"

His hips levered forward at her insistent pulling. The spittle-wet tip of his cock touched her nether lips. They both shuddered. And then the woman shrieked with joy when Slocum pushed on forward, burying himself to the hilt within her tightly clenching interior.

"Do it," she sobbed. "You are so much. Do it now. I am afire with need."

Slocum retreated slowly, savoring the sensations

mounting in his own body. The woman reached out and cupped his asscheeks to pull him back forward. But he resisted.

"I don't even know your name," he said. "Mine's John."

"John. Oh, yes, John. Now!"

"Your name," he said, not giving in even though his body screamed at him for the denial.

"Juliana. I am Juliana, and I need you!"

Slocum felt like a dam getting ready to bust wide open. He jerked every time Juliana touched him, her nails raking, her fingers soothing and exciting, her lips pressing into his chest and throat and neck as they struggled together on the creaking hotel bed. The pressures got too much for him. His hips levered forward powerfully, and he ground his groin into hers.

Juliana tossed her head and let out a low animal moan of pure pleasure. Her entire body convulsed with ecstasy just seconds before he erupted and spilled his seed into her grasping hot interior.

Slocum sank down beside the woman, arms wrapped around her. She nuzzled in close and ran her fingers through the mat of hair on his chest.

"You are not like most men," she said.

"Funny," said Slocum. "You're the first woman who's ever accused me of that."

"Oh, that is not what I mean," Juliana said, her eyes going wide. "I meant you are different from most American men. You are . . ."

Before Juliana had a chance to finish, a man kicked in the door of the room. He stood in the doorway, revolver leveled at them.

"Where is it?" he demanded.

"You caught me with my pants down," Slocum

said, sitting up in bed and gallantly shielding Juliana's naked body from the intruder's view. "Mind telling me what you want?"

The man cocked the heavy pistol and aimed it directly between Slocum's eyes. "Jade box. I want it."

Slocum frowned. This man's accent was not as pronounced as the sailor's, but it was still apparent. Another Russian. And he wanted the jade pianoforte miniature, too.

"I don't have it," Slocum lied.

"Then you die unless you tell me where it is."

"Please," Juliana said. "Let me put on my dress. This is indecent!"

The gunman sneered. He gestured to the pile of clothes draped over the chair. He reached out first, though, and removed Slocum's Colt and tossed it into the far corner of the room. The man's expression turned to a leer when Juliana unashamedly went to the clothing and began dressing.

The man's attention was diverted, but Slocum decided there wasn't a hell of a lot he could do. He couldn't get untangled from the sheets in time to do much but get himself ventilated. Reaching his gun was out of the question. When the gunman had thrown it to the other side of the room, it had skittered under a small dresser.

Slocum studied this robber and knew doing anything but giving up the jade miniature would be a mistake. The man was burly, with arms half again the size of Slocum's. The weathered face had seen hardship and sported scars that gleamed in the dim light of the hotel room. There was something slightly odd about the clothing, but Slocum couldn't place it. Most telling was the hint of a Russian accent. He wondered if Stephan had confessed the loss of the jade box to his superiors and they'd sent this man around to retrieve the precious artifact.

It didn't much matter to Slocum. All he wanted was to get rid of the gunman and the heavy pistol he pointed so carelessly.

"What's so damn important about that box?" he asked. "It's valuable, but is it worth killing for?"

The man turned and faced Slocum. Juliana had almost finished dressing, and that show was at an end. The man nervously swiped at his thick handlebar mustache and nodded. The fanatical light in his eyes told Slocum all he needed to know. To recover that jade box this man would kill half of San Francisco.

"Just asking," Slocum said amiably.

The roar of the .41 derringer discharging deafened Slocum, but it didn't stop him from moving like greased lightning. The bullet hit the man in the side and drove him into the wall. Slocum vaulted from the bed and swung, his fist sinking into the man's stomach all the way to the wrist. The lack of air exploding from the lungs told Slocum that he was too late—the gunman had died almost instantly from the .41 slug.

"Good shooting," Slocum said to Juliana. The woman held his derringer in a rock-steady hand. And the double-barreled pistol was aimed at him now.

"I am a crack shot," she said in a low voice. "Do not make me prove it by shooting you too, John. I have come to care for you a great deal. It would be a pity to lose you so soon."

"Juliana, point that in some other direction," Slocum said. But he stood frozen. He knew when someone was running a bluff and when someone meant what they said. The lovely dark-haired woman meant it when she said she'd kill him if he didn't cooperate.

"The jade pianoforte," she said. "I want it. Is it with your clothing? It must be." Blue eyes never leaving him, Juliana rummaged through his clothing, checking the trousers first, then the shirt. She found the wad of bills and discarded them without so much as a second glance. The three-inch-long miniature tumbled out of his other shirt pocket. Juliana smiled and put it away safely in the soft folds of her velvet skirt.

"What's going on?" Slocum asked. "You kill this owlhoot with my own gun, then you rob me."

"Is this such a blow to your vanity?" she asked. "You wonder how anyone can make love to you and then do such a thing?"

"Something like that," he said, playing for time. If he kept Juliana talking long enough she'd make a mistake.

"You are a remarkable man, John. It is too bad we did not meet under better circumstances. You will climb back into the bed. Now!"

He obeyed. Juliana retrieved his Colt, wrapped it in his clothing, and tucked the bundle under her arm.

"Do not attempt to follow me. Please believe me when I say I mean you no harm. But I will kill you if you become involved in matters that do not concern you. Goodbye, my love. You *were* good." Juliana flashed him a dazzling smile, then slipped out the door, closing it behind her.

Slocum sat on the bed, his anger mounting. No one pushed John Slocum around. Not like this.

3

Slocum sat in the middle of the rumpled sheets and stewed for a few seconds, then vaulted out of bed and went to the small window looking out onto Drum Street. He had to rub away some of the dirt caked on the pane, but he made out Juliana hurrying down the deserted, foggy street. She paused under one of the gas lamps and tossed the bundle of his clothes into the gutter. Slocum heard the faint rattle of his Colt Peacemaker hitting cobblestone and shuddered. He lived by that gun and didn't like seeing it mistreated.

Struggling with the window, he got it raised and started to climb out and follow Juliana when a cold breeze off San Francisco Bay nearly froze the flesh from his bones. Slocum laughed at himself. He had forgotten he was naked. Even though it was damn near three in the morning and the streets were empty of most all law-abiding citizens, it wouldn't pay to be caught by one of the roving bands of specials. There'd be no way to explain to them what had happened.

Slocum lowered the window and then caught sight of the gunman's hand flopped back on the floor.

"You weren't much good alive. Leastways, you'll give me something now that you're dead." Slocum set to stripping off the clothing and found it more difficult than he'd imagined. The corpse didn't co-operate at all.

The man was much heavier than Slocum and had shorter arms and legs. Slocum looked like a clown in a traveling circus, but he was at least dressed now. The dead man's gun had ended up beneath his body. It felt awkward in Slocum's grip. He examined the pistol and tried to remember if he'd ever seen one like it before.

He hadn't.

"Won't need it for long," he said to the dead man. Slocum had tried on the man's boots and found them too small by several sizes. He padded out on bare feet, down the hall, down the stairs, out the front. The desk clerk slumped over his ledger, snoring loudly. If the single fatal shot hadn't awakened the sleeping clerk, Slocum wasn't about to do a lot of needless explaining.

He walked quickly down the street, the cold stone underfoot adding speed to his movement. Slocum scooped up the parcel where Juliana had abandoned it, found his gun and checked it out, and noted with some surprise that she hadn't bothered to take the roll of greenbacks from his shirt pocket. Even in the room she had disdainfully ignored them. The jade pianoforte miniature was all that seemed to matter to her.

Or maybe this was Juliana's way of thanking him for getting her the jade box.

Slocum put on his boots and stalked off to find another hotel. When the dead man was found in his room, Slocum wanted to be far away. In the Barbary Coast nobody much cared about such things, but he didn't want to spend a lot of time telling the city police he couldn't answer their questions.

Who was the dead man? A Russian from his accent

and the odd pistol he carried, but who? Why had he wanted the jade box? Why had Juliana? Other than it was worth a few hundred dollars, why kill for it?

Slocum wanted the answer to an even more important question: Where did he find Juliana? San Francisco wasn't that big a place. Sooner or later he'd track her down. Then questions would be answered. Questions just begging for answers.

"Looking for a Russian, about six inches shorter than me, bushy handlebar mustache, heavyset." Slocum described the dead man the best he could. The barkeep at McGuire's just walked off, not answering. Everyone Slocum asked either drank his whiskey and told him nothing or became openly hostile.

"A word of advice, bucko," said Sean McGuire, overhearing the latest of Slocum's attempts to get information. "The Barbary Coast ain't the place to go nosin' about with a passel of questions. People been known to just vanish, like."

Slocum nodded, asking, "The man's a Russian. Where would I find another one to talk to?"

"The whole city's filthy with the Russkies. Always has been. Russian Hill, now there's a fine place to build a house. Not too far distant is the Russian River. Even a colony of the bastards near Bodega Bay. Fort Ross, they're callin' it. But look around," the jovial Irishman said. "They're everywhere."

Slocum knew better than to press his luck. He thanked McGuire and left the saloon, his steps going toward the harbor. Ships from the Orient docked in San Francisco and returned to their home ports daily. The Bay was a major stopping point for all Pacific trade routes. Slocum perched on one of the rotting pilings of a dock, tried to ignore the smell of dead fish, and studied the names of the ships. Only when he came to one in Russian script did he pause.

He knew nothing more than the names Georgi and Stephan and that they'd arrived the morning before on a ship from Russia. Slocum decided he had nothing to lose asking after them. He wanted information on the jade box and why it was important enough to kill for.

Find the box, find Juliana.

Slocum looked over the steamship and decided this might be the one. Brass fittings on the sides were brightly polished, and the smokestack showed signs of having recently been overhauled. One spar had been mended, and a considerable amount of new line had been put aboard. Slocum remembered how Stephan had mentioned that his ship had been caught up in a fierce winter storm and had sustained heavy damage. All that Slocum saw was in keeping with a ship being repaired and put back into seaworthy condition.

He looked around and saw only a few dock wallopers lounging nearby. They looked to be more interested in a bottle they were passing around than in anything else. Slocum didn't think his questions would set well with any of them. It had been hard enough in McGuire's. Here it might prove fatal if he stepped on the wrong toes.

Slocum hitched up his gunbelt and took the thong off the hammer of his Colt, just to be sure. The Barbary Coast was no fit place to walk about unarmed. On the waterfront it was even less hospitable, from what he'd seen.

Going up the gangplank, Slocum hailed the deck officer. A dour Russian dressed in a heavy woolen jacket and a cap with a spattering of gold braid on it watched him all the way up.

"What do you want?" the officer demanded in heavily accented English. "This not passenger ship."

"Might want to sign on as a hand," said Slocum.

"You are not sailor."

"True," admitted Slocum, "but I'm looking for a couple buddies of mine I met ashore the other night. Stephan and Georgi."

"What are surnames?" the officer asked gruffly. "All sailors are having names Georgi and Stephan."

"Can't say I ever heard them." Slocum saw the anger building in the officer. His swarthy face clouded over and a stubby finger shot out, pressing hard into Slocum's chest.

"You leave *Resheemast* now," he said. His finger drove harder into Slocum's chest and pushed him back a half step.

"That the name of your ship?" Slocum asked, trying to derail the anger and failing.

"Off!"

"Not too hospitable a cuss, are you?" Slocum said. The officer wasn't content with Slocum's speed in leaving and shoved him—hard.

Slocum stumbled, came up in a crouch, then swung with all his might. His fist connected squarely with the Russian officer's belly. The man grunted and staggered a pace, then let out a bull-throated roar as he charged.

Slocum found himself caught up in a bear hug that crushed the air from his lungs and threatened to break his back. Each gasp he made allowed the Russian to tighten up, preventing that much more air from entering his lungs. Blackness swirled in his head and threatened to consume him. Slocum swung the palms of his hands and clapped hard on the Russian's ears.

The smack sounded loud to Slocum. To the Russian

it had to be both deafening and painful. He yelped and released his hold. Slocum took in deep lungfuls of air and regained his strength. The attack had taken him by surprise. Now he knew what he faced.

The officer rubbed his ears and started forward again, murder burning hotly in his eyes.

"Don't," was all Slocum said. His Peacemaker had come easily to hand and was now cocked and pointed straight for the man.

Slocum wondered if the sailor would have kept coming if there hadn't been a sharp command in Russian that stopped him dead in his tracks. He swung about, stared up at the bridge, saluted, and went off, giving Slocum a glance over his shoulder that would have frozen a heated branding iron.

"Much obliged, Captain," Slocum called out.

"Please to leave my ship at once."

The captain didn't even stay to see if Slocum obeyed. He whirled and stormed off.

With no other sailors in sight, Slocum decided it best to drop it and go see if he could find Stephan somewhere else. There wasn't even any assurance that the Russian had shipped on this particular boat. Slocum ran a hand through his black hair, shook his head, then put his Stetson back on. For a second he wondered if all this was worth it. The Russians had bad tempers and were more likely to fight than talk, and he could only end up getting his head split open if he hung around overlong.

"Damnit, no," he said to himself, staring up at the foreign steamer. He had almost been killed twice over that jade box—three times, if he wanted to count Juliana, and he probably should—and he had to find out more. Being robbed was a part of it, but his curiosity ran rampant now. How had a lowly deckhand like Stephan come by the expensive box in the first place?

Why were all those Russians trying to kill him?

Not for the first time, Slocum thought back on the time spent with Juliana. Another piece missing from the completed picture. The woman was an enigma, lovely, mysteriously coming out of the fog and into his bed with an expertise that still made him feel warm in the crotch. She wasn't American, of that he was sure. Yet she didn't have the heavy Russian accent the others did either. What the lovely, dark-haired Juliana did have was his jade box.

Slocum poked about on the docks, listening more than talking, and found out nothing at all. The Russian ship had been docked at the right time, but no one had heard of either Georgi or Stephan, not that this surprised him very much. He hung around, waiting and watching. Sooner or later one of the two sailors would show up. When he did, Slocum had questions to ask.

At dusk, just as Slocum was tiring of the vigil, he saw a flash of white as a man moved down the gangplank of the *Resheemast*. The sailor wore the usual dark wool pea coat, but the white silk scarf around his neck had come from China, Slocum guessed. It was too fine a product for the Russian to come by otherwise.

Slocum followed, but the sailor quickly detected him and spun around, knife in hand.

"What you doing behind me?" Georgi demanded.

"My name's Slocum. We met last night. At McGuire's. Your friend Stephan's the one I want to talk to. Where can I find him?"

"Stephan?" the Russian asked, as if hearing the name for the first time. The tone was all right, but the frightened expression on the man's face told a different story.

"Your friend with the jade box. The miniature pianoforte. You remember, don't you, Georgi?"

"I know nothing of this. Go away!"

Slocum stepped forward, twisted sideways, and let the knife slide past him harmlessly. He grabbed the sailor's brawny wrist and jerked as hard as he could. The knife went flying off, hit a piling, and sank into the Bay.

"Now that you're more peaceable," Slocum said, "I want some answers. Where's Stephan?"

"Please, no, he is dead!"

Slocum frowned.

"He is!" insisted the sailor. "They kill him for what he did. They not know I have anything to do with stealing."

"The jade box belonged to the captain?"

"Captain Kerensky? That *starookha?* That old woman? Ha!"

"Then who?" demanded Slocum.

"I cannot tell you."

"They killed Stephan," Slocum pointed out, not even knowing who "they" were. "They'll kill you, too, if I keep poking around. Give me some answers and I'll butt out."

"You will?" Georgi thought this over. "You have no other interest?"

"None," Slocum assured him.

For the first time the sailor relaxed a little. Slocum kept alert, however. He had seen too many men use such a trick to cut and run.

"Very well. I tell you, but you cannot speak of this to anyone else."

"I promise that much," said Slocum.

"Good. The jade box, it comes from fine St. Petersburg company of Fabergé."

"This Fabergé made the box?"

"He is best goldsmith in world," said Georgi. "He even make—"

Slocum had his Colt out and cocked when Georgi stiffened. The man's sentence had cut off too abruptly, and Slocum saw why. Georgi spun slowly, as if trying to corkscrew himself into the rotting wood dock. A bone-handled knife protruded from the center of his back. Georgi hit hard on the dock, but Slocum hadn't stayed around to watch. He dove for cover behind bales piled to his left.

Straining as hard as he could, all the man heard close by were the gentle protests of wooden hulls as the Bay lifted and dropped the ships on its tide. In the distance came the screeches of hungry seagulls and a mournful foghorn signaling the coming of a fog bank.

Slocum stood and looked around. The twilight had deepened to the point that he wouldn't be able to see Georgi's killer even if the man was standing ten feet away.

Moving as quietly as he could, Slocum tried to get a better look at the spot where Georgi's murderer must have stood to throw the knife. The only warning Slocum had was the scrape of leather on wood. He bent double, twisted around, and thrust out his Colt, ready to fire.

The knife barely missed his right ear. The blade sank into a bale waiting to be loaded aboard a ship. Slocum held his fire. He had no good target and didn't want to reveal his exact position by the flash of his Colt.

"Owwww," he moaned, faking injury. Slocum made a few sounds intended to convince his assailant that the knife had found its target. He fell heavily to the dock, making as much racket as he could, then silently shifted position and waited.

A dark form drifted out of a doorway. The bright flash of a knife blade told Slocum that the would-be assassin had come prepared for a long fight. If he carried three knives, he might have four. Slocum sighted carefully, waited for the dark figure to be framed by two stacks of cargo, then fired. The way the man snapped upright and fell face down convinced Slocum that his bullet had flown true.

He knelt beside the man and saw that the bullet had entered the left temple and killed instantly.

"Damn," Slocum cursed. Then he cursed his own stupidity when a gaffing hook slid forth and hooked his gun hand. The sharp point cut into his wrist and forced him to drop his Colt.

There'd been more than one man listening to what he and Georgi had said.

Slocum used his left hand to grip the shaft of the hook and keep it from gouging deeper into his wrist. He yanked and got it free from the hidden assailant's grip.

But Slocum was still faced with the problem of not knowing where the next attack might come from or who was doing the bushwhacking. He searched around for his gun and found it.

Bleeding from the wound on his wrist, Slocum remembered all he had been taught in the Confederate army. Find the high ground. Use it for sniping. During the war he had been one of the South's finest snipers. He climbed up on the top of a stack of crates and lay

prone, searching through the forest of boxes for some
sign of the man who had used the gaffing hook on
him.

Nothing.

Slocum strained to hear. Nothing moved. He took
a few minutes to clumsily bind his wounded wrist.
Flexing his hand convinced him that he wasn't too
badly hurt. He still could hold his Colt. Slocum returned to his vigil. Aboard one of the docked ships,
sailors began singing a bawdy chanty. Elsewhere men
came and went in search of liquor and female com-
panionship.

He knew that he might shoot the wrong one if he
stayed here much longer. Slocum hated to give up
when a potential backshooter was still alive, but he
had no other choice. Climbing down from the crates,
he again stood on the dock, listening, waiting for the
knife or bullet that never came.

Slocum retreated, moving cautiously, then hurrying until he melted into the throngs near Portsmouth
Square. The men shouting for the attention of pro-
spective customers in their melodeons, whores bla-
tantly propositioning passersby, the rumble of carriages
in the street, the preachers delivering their hellfire and
brimstone prophecies—all these rose and surrounded
Slocum, giving a more comfortable feel. Slocum found
himself a deadfall and entered, stepping over a pair
of men who had passed out from too much liquor. He
shuffled through the sawdust on the floor, found an
empty table, and ordered whiskey.

He got trade whiskey but drank it anyway. Slocum
needed the hot, raw warmth it gave him.

As he drank he worked over all that had happened.
By the time he had finished four stiff drinks he decided

that he wasn't interested enough in the jade box to keep looking.

Not with Georgi dead, and probably Stephan, too. And Georgi's killer on the dock. And whoever the Russian was that Juliana had shot in the hotel room the night before. Four dead over a bauble, even an expensive one, was too much. Rather than find more dead bodies, Slocum would let the entire matter drop here and now.

It galled him, but he'd do it.

Slocum even considered the proposition of the scrawny, red-headed "pretty waiter girl" when she told him she was available for only four bits. It'd help him forget all that had happened, he reckoned. Nothing else seemed to be working, and this might do the trick. He followed the redhead upstairs to her crib, watched as she undressed, then lowered his drawers and climbed aboard.

But the distraction didn't drive away the memory of what had happened. All the while he was screwing hell out of the whore he thought of Juliana.

4

Slocum kept to himself for the next few days, choosing to gamble in deadfalls and saloons other than McGuire's. The big Irishman wouldn't take kindly to people getting shot up in his establishment, and Slocum would like it even less if he were the one being shot. As long as he didn't know who it was stalking him through the San Francisco streets, he had no chance of fighting back.

By finding new places to drink and gamble, he avoided most of those problems. Slocum didn't think he was important enough for a real manhunt. Stephan had been killed because he lost the jade box, and Georgi had a habit of talking to people he shouldn't have. And Slocum doubted the one man he had killed on the dock meant much to those involved in this mind-twisting battle.

He preferred being on his own, being left alone. Slocum's only reason for staying in San Francisco even a day longer was to parlay his six hundred dollars into a real wad. He wanted enough greenbacks to choke a cow. Then he'd be on his way, north to Oregon, north to the serenity of the Pacific Northwest's forests and mountains.

"Dealer takes one," the man across the table said. Slocum eyed him and decided the man was running a bluff.

"Stand," he said. Slocum didn't have squat, but then neither did the dealer. And only the pair of them stayed in for the large pot. Slocum watched the nervous tic developing at the corner of the man's mouth and knew he had him.

"Fold," said the dealer.

"Thanks."

"What do you have?" asked the dealer. He wiped sweat off his upper lip.

"You have to pay for the privilege. You folded," said Slocum. Showing anyone the worthless hand didn't strike him as good sense. If the others got to know the habit of his play, it made winning that much harder in future games.

"Show me."

"Don't get riled," said Slocum. He scooped up the money from the table and put it into his pockets. "Let me buy you a drink."

"You just took most of my money," the man said, half rising from his chair.

"You're lucky that's all he took, Sam," said one of the man's friends standing behind him. "Take his liquor and let's go. This place is starting to give me the gollywobbles. Too closed in."

"You miners, too?" asked Slocum.

"Yeah, what's it to you?" demanded the man who had dealt.

"Been out in the Sierras for damn near six months myself. Luck wasn't very good there. Improved a mite in San Francisco," said Slocum, taking any sting he could out of the other man's losing. Slocum had tired early on with men not owning up to their losses. The Russian sailor's losing the jade box had caused Slocum a world of trouble he had neither asked for nor wanted.

"We did good in the hills," said the other man. "Come on, Sam, take his liquor."

Slocum drank with the other miners, buying two more rounds, then they all left the deadfall together. They split and went in different directions outside, which suited Slocum just fine. He blinked at the bright sunlight. He had been gambling all night long and felt the strain now. Slocum turned tiredly in the direction of his hotel—and that's when he heard the excitement of crowds gathering in the street ahead.

California Street was packed with spectators hopping up and down trying to see over the heads of those in front of them. Slocum stayed at the rear of the crowd, cursing the delay. So many people thronged the street that it would be impossible to cross it and get to his hotel. Best to wait and let the crowd thin down.

"What's the commotion?" he asked a man wearing a cutaway jacket and a silk cravat with a diamond stickpin. For so early in the morning, the man was dressed fit to kill.

"Where have you been, sir?" the gussied-up man asked. "Count Borov, emissary from the court of Tsar Alexander III, is visiting our fair city."

Slocum nodded, saying nothing.

"This is a great occasion. It is the first time such a state visit has been made since Director Tebenkov left in 1850."

"Director of what?"

"Why, the Russian-American Company, of course." The man looked at Slocum with some disdain. "Surely you have heard of the Russian-American Company?"

"Of course," said Slocum. He hadn't.

"My father was a trade commissioner. I have the honor of being a delegate to this trade mission."

"You supposed to be in a parade?"

"There will be a parade later. Count Borov will go to the Russian consulate, where we will meet."

"Why aren't you up front, where you can get a better look?" asked Slocum.

"It is my duty to negotiate, not to gawk, sir."

Slocum edged away, wondering if the man weren't another of the refugees from Bedlam that seemed to gather in San Francisco. Slocum had heard of a self-proclaimed Emperor Norton who had written to both Abraham Lincoln and Jefferson Davis offering his support during the war. Lincoln had thanked him, and Jeff Davis had asked for a donation for the Southern cause.

The sounds of carriage wheels rattling along the street quieted the crowd. One woman grabbed the arm of the man with her and shook it, saying, "There he is! Isn't he the handsomest man you've ever seen?" Her male companion silenced her with a black look.

Curious, Slocum straightened and peered over the crowd. An ornately appointed carriage slowly rolled along. In the open back sat a man more gaudily dressed than a color-blind peacock. His chest was littered with gold and silver medals and ribbons of every rainbow hue. A gold sword balanced on the man's left side, and at his right was a highly polished leather holster, the flap hiding the contents. Slocum didn't doubt that the pistol inside was gleaming too—but more from polishing than use. Highly waxed mustaches swirled out to fine tips, and the dark eyes showed no hint of pleasure at being in this parade.

Slocum decided this Count Borov could be very cruel if he set his mind to it.

He started to turn away and work his way around the people in the street when the occupant of a second carriage caught Slocum's eye. He stopped and stared, his teeth grinding slightly at what he saw.

"Juliana," he muttered.

The dark-haired woman rode behind the Count's carriage in one only slightly less resplendent. She wore a bright blue velvet dress with the same fur trim that had graced her blouse the night she had stolen the jade box. Delicate white lace decorated the hem of her skirt, and Juliana waved to the crowd while holding linen gloves in her left hand.

Slocum started pushing his way to the front of the crowd. Suddenly a loud roar swept along California Street. The people around him were thrown off their feet with contemptuous ease. Slocum stayed on his feet, but the explosion stunned him.

He wobbled as if drunk, then supported himself against a building. Confused thoughts of earthquakes ran through his mind, then the world settled down for him. He ran one hand over his damp forehead; the hand came away bloody. The explosion had sent pieces of debris flying, and one had scratched him.

Slocum heard the frightened whinnying of horses and saw Juliana's carriage being reined to one side of the street, the driver brutally whipping the animal to a dead gallop. The carriage raced past the smoking ruins of Count Borov's vehicle.

Already police were swarming forward, liberally using their clubs and foot-long knives to hold back the crowd. Slocum advanced more cautiously and saw the crater left in the street.

"A bomb," he heard one cop say to another. "The bastards blew up the Count."

"Is he dead?" called out Slocum.

"Of course he is, you fool," answered one of the nearby policemen.

"And Juliana? How is she?"

"Who?"

"The woman in the second carriage," Slocum said.

"Don't know nothing about her. Damn, but what a mess those sons of bitches make for us. Look at that."

Slocum wasn't squeamish, not after the war and all the killing and dismemberment he had seen then, but this wasn't a pretty sight. The bomb had gone off at precisely the right instant—the wrong one for the Count. The blast had surged straight up through the bottom of the carriage and hadn't left even one of his medals intact. Of his body there was only a bloody trace.

"Why can't they stay home and do this to each other?" complained another cop. "No, they gotta come to San Francisco and mess up our streets."

The police began pushing back the crowd, Slocum with it. He struggled through the crush and found himself standing in the mouth of an alleyway. He heaved a deep breath and shook his head. Fate wasn't playing fair with him. He had finally accumulated enough in winnings to head out of town, and then he had to see Juliana again. Whether it was damaged pride at what she had done to him or simple curiosity—wanting to know what all this was about—Slocum couldn't rightly say.

He just knew he wasn't going to leave San Francisco until he had again spoken to Juliana.

"So she rides in parades with Russian counts who get their asses blown up. What else does she do, I wonder?"

Slocum waited until the stunned but still curious crowd dispersed, then crossed California Street and went on to the hotel where he had stayed since that

night with Juliana. He entered—and didn't see the
three men following him. Two stayed in front of the
hotel while the third went to the rear. They did nothing
the rest of the day, choosing only to wait and watch,
and when Slocum again emerged at sunset, the three
trailed closely behind.

Slocum had rested and spent a good deal of the
day thinking about what he ought to do to find Juliana.
Nothing obvious suggested itself, short of showing up
at the Russian consulate office and demanding to see
her. But what if Juliana weren't even her real name?
He guessed from the treatment accorded her that she
must be some sort of Russian nobility. Slocum bought
a *San Francisco Bulletin* from a street vendor and read
through the details of the assassination.

"Count Borov, I knew that," he muttered to himself
as he read. "All the gory details and nothing about
the others in the parade." Slocum dropped the newspaper into the gutter and walked on.

Behind, a scuffed boot stirred the newspaper in the
mud. The three men glanced at the headlines, ex-
changed solemn looks, then continued behind Slocum.

Slocum wandered along the street until a saloon at
the northern end of Meigg's Wharf caught his eye.
The Cobweb Palace had a steady stream of patrons
entering and leaving. Slocum went in and then stopped,
staring at the interior. The decor was totally unlike
anything he had seen—or expected, even in a place
like San Francisco. The interior was a mass of cobwebs hanging in festoons from the walls and ceilings.
Even the lighting fixtures and decorations were
shrouded by the feathery spiders' nests. Slocum walked
to the bar and wondered if any liquor at all was served.
From the way the cobwebs dangled from the necks

of the whiskey bottles behind the bar, he doubted it.

"What'll it be?" asked the barkeep.

"Rye."

As he was being served, Slocum heard raucous cries of parrots, monkeys, and other small animals. Peering into the gloom along the ceiling, he saw rows of dangling cages.

"Grandfather Warner, Grandfather Warner," squawked one brightly colored parrot, swooping down to the bar and drinking from a glass still half filled with whiskey. It then cut loose a string of invective that startled Slocum.

"Swears a blue streak in four languages," the barkeep told Slocum.

"I gathered that," said Slocum, sipping at the watered drink. "Those are paintings behind the cobwebs?" he asked, making out the forms of nude women.

"And a few walrus tusks and sperm-whale teeth. Abe Warner had them carved up right nice, with patriotic scenes. Take a look at 'em before you go," said the barkeep.

Slocum turned to examine one of the tusks all but hidden under the cobwebs. That was when he saw the three men enter by the front way. He wouldn't have paid any notice if one hadn't grabbed the other's arm to keep him from pointing—at Slocum.

Slocum sat at a table, the chair reasonably clean of cobwebs. The three went to the bar. One of them ordered a hot toddy and was served a boiling mess of whiskey, gin, and cloves that made Slocum's nose wrinkle, even at this distance. The man drank it as if it were good. The two other men with him drank nothing, however, and this further alerted Slocum.

He finished his watery rye whiskey, rose, and quickly left. He crossed the street and waited. Seconds

later the three rushed from the Cobweb Palace, looking frantically up and down the street for some sign
of Slocum.

Slocum studied the three carefully, a cold chill
settling in his belly. At first glance they seemed like
any other patrons of any other bar. Now Slocum wasn't
so sure about that. They stood uncharacteristically
close together and spoke in guarded tones. Something
about their clothing pegged them as foreigners, although what it might be Slocum couldn't say. From
their interest in him, Slocum figured they must be
Russians.

Whole damn town's full of them, he thought. *Can't
go out without stepping on two of them and disturbing
another.*

They split up, two going left and the other right.
Slocum fell in behind the solitary man and tracked
him to the corner. There he grabbed him by the collar
and swung him into a doorway, slamming him hard
against a wall.

"Why are you following me?" Slocum demanded.

"I know nothing," the man said. The Russian accent came through so thick Slocum could cut it with
a knife.

"Who sent you?"

"I know nothing."

Slocum tried to loosen the man's tongue with a
hard fist to the belly. The man only doubled over; he
didn't seem any closer to talking. Slocum checked to
see if anyone in the street had noticed. On the far side
two policemen walked their beat. Soon enough the
man's two friends would come looking for him. Slocum walked off, not bothering to question him further.
He made several quick turns, cut back, waited in a
shadowy doorway. Only when he was satisfied that

he had lost the men tracking him did Slocum head back into the Barbary Coast section of town.

He had decided to ignore the loss of the exquisitely wrought jade box and forget about Juliana—but that had been before the count was blown up this morning and the three hoodlums had started following him. While Slocum knew it was foolish to do anything but hightail it away from San Francisco and head for territory more amicable, he was getting madder and madder at the way the Russians treated him. Worst of all was not knowing what was going on.

Count Borov blown up. Juliana in the parade after having stolen the box. The sailors dead. The gunfight on the docks.

"I'll find out," he said in a grim tone.

The only way Slocum could think of to get some notion as to what the tangle of events meant was to return to the dockside saloons and look for the ones catering to Russian sailors. He made certain the thong was pulled off the hammer of his Colt before entering a likely looking place. The paint peeled from the sign on Pacific Street between Drum and Davis, but Slocum made out that this was Kelly's Saloon and Boardinghouse. A dozen hungry-looking men hung about the front door. One of them hurried forward and took Slocum by the elbow, guiding him to one side.

"Mate, you just in port?"

"Not a sailor," Slocum said, pulling free of the man's grip.

"Don't make no never mind," he was assured. "Mr. Kelly's good to all men. You been workin' the goldfields?" Sharp, shrewd eyes noted the calluses on Slocum's hands.

"Didn't have any luck," Slocum said.

"All the more reason to let Mr. Kelly buy you a

drink. Why, it's been said that he serves the best damn Pisco Punch this side of the Bank Exchange."

Slocum doubted this claim. The Bank Exchange on Montgomery and California was a swank saloon catering to prominent businessmen. He had passed by it and shunned the marble flooring and the fancy-ass oil paintings inside.

"Get many Russian sailors in Kelly's?" asked Slocum.

"Does that make a difference?"

"Want to meet up with some. Made friends and then lost track of them."

The runner gave Slocum a broad wink, as if saying, "Whatever you like, we can provide, no matter how depraved."

The man escorted Slocum into the saloon. Slocum was surprised to find it more neatly kept than most. The constant swishing of the tide under the floor bothered him a little, the saloon being built on a pier out over the Bay, but he soon got used to it. Slocum figured the sailors found this place to be just like home.

"Here's my good friend," the runner said, slapping Slocum on the back and pushing him up to the bar. "Duncan, my man, a drink for him. On Mr. Kelly's special account."

Slocum watched as the barkeep passed over two dollars to the runner, then went to mix the drink. He had heard of such places. The runners were responsible for bringing in patrons, and in this section of town that usually meant sailors. Some runners would take Whitehall boats out to ships just lowering anchor and swarm over the railings, almost dragging the sailors off their ships. Fights sometimes broke out between the runners from rival saloons—bloody fights ending in death and maiming.

Slocum slowly looked around. He didn't doubt Mr. Kelly could clean out a sailor in the span of an hour at those gambling tables. Each one had at least two cardsharps working in cahoots to bilk the other players. And if an hour wasn't enough, the boardinghouse portion of the three-story structure would erase the rest of the hard-earned sea pay.

High prices for rooms and food, maybe a whore thrown in, and the sailor would be in debt again.

The barkeep dropped a colorless, fragrant drink in front of Slocum.

He waved away any money when Slocum went to pay, saying, "As Lonzo said, this'n's on Mr. Kelly."

Slocum sampled the Pisco Punch and found it mild, with a slight fruit taste. The burned aftertaste reminded him of Scotch whiskey, but it was more delicate than that.

"Good," he said. "But I insist on paying."

The barkeep shrugged. "When you're ready, I'll fix you another one."

"How much?"

"Two bits." Slocum blinked. This was steep, even for a drink this good. He reached into his vest pocket and pulled out the coin. For a moment, he hesitated, trying to drop it onto the bar. Slocum noticed he was starting to weave a bit.

"Strong. Take your time, mister. Even the best of 'em can't put away more'n three or four Piscos."

"What goes into it?"

"Trade secret," the barkeep said. "Course, the main ingredient is Pisco brandy, distilled from La Rosa del Peru and shipped straight up the coast in those fancy five-gallon earthen jugs. The rest of what goes in, never mind that. Drink hearty."

Slocum bided his time, sipping slowly at the brandy punch, trying to engage some of the Russian sailors in conversation. Mostly he failed at this and contented himself with listening. While he didn't speak Russian, words and names came to him. Count Borov was mentioned often, but not once did he hear the name Juliana.

"Everyone makin' you feel right at home, mister?" came a jovial voice. Slocum blinked. A tall man in a brocade jacket stood next to him. "I'm Kelly. Owner of this dive."

"Pleased to meet you." Slocum felt oddly disconnected from his body, as if part of him floated a few feet away. The brandy punch was stronger than he'd thought.

"Don't see your likes in here often."

"Looking for work," Slocum lied. "Those fellows lurking outside don't seem to be doing much for you."

"The runners? Slow time for them. Been slow ever since I lost Johnny Devine." Kelly squinted at Slocum and said, "You aren't the kind of bloke I'd expect to be hanging around like this. Lonzo said you have a yen for Russian sailors. Seen you tryin' to spark conversation with a couple of them. Close mouthed lot, they are."

"Trying to find a friend," Slocum said. His mind moved in spurts now.

"If'n he's a Russkie, this is a good place to look right now. Couple Russian steamers hove into port in the past week."

"Count Borov's ship?" he asked.

"Have a cigar," said Kelly. He reached into his pocket and drew out a thick, tobacco-leaf-rolled masterpiece. Even the Havanas Slocum favored when he could afford them didn't look or smell as fine. "My special blend, made just for me."

Slocum bit the end off, spat, and let Kelly light it for him. He inhaled deeply and instantly tasted the difference.

He exhaled and asked, "What's in this?" Thick cloying smoke curled up under his nose and made his eyes water. The room began spinning even faster than it had before.

"Most men pass out from the Pisco Punch," Kelly said in an offhand manner. "One puff on that stogie usually drops the rest. You must have the constitution of a bull."

"What is it?" asked Slocum. The room began to collapse into a single spot in front of his eyes. All else turned inky black.

"Those are made special for me by a Chinese cigar maker. Just a bit of opium in it. I call it my Shanghai smoke."

Mocking laughter filled Slocum's ears. It was the last thing he heard before collapsing face down on the table.

5

"Twenty dollars!" someone shouted. "You bleedin' crimp! Try to rob me like that, will you?"

Slocum stirred and felt as if the top of his head was going to fall off. He lay face down on a smelly wood plank, his arms and legs leaden. He tried to piece everything together, and only slowly did it come back to him.

He had been drinking in the waterfront dive. Kelly's. The Pisco Punch. The cigar. The cigar!

What had Kelly said? Made special for him in China. He was being shanghaied!

Slocum's blood began churning faster and faster, anger at what had happened giving him strength. He forced open heavily lidded eyes and focused. The best he could reckon, he was in the hold of a ship anchored in San Francisco Bay. The rocking motion, the salt and fish odors, the dampness all around made this seem like the right answer.

Shanghaied.

Slocum had heard the stories but never paid much mind to them. He was used to the wide-open plains and mountains, trapping beaver and hunting buffalo and deer. The dangers there were from the elements and the Indians, the occasional road agents, and even from not quite honest lawmen. That was his world, and he knew the people in it. Too late he realized he

54

should never have gotten involved with the Russian sailors, with trying to locate Juliana and the jade box. It took him too far afield, and now he was paying the price.

"Never wanted to see China," he muttered. His voice caught in his throat, and his mouth felt as if someone had stuffed it with long-staple Louisiana cotton.

He rolled onto his side and looked up to see two men arguing. The one protested the price—of Slocum and the other men—being sold into slavery.

"But Cap'n, these are *fine* men. Strong, willing to work."

"Last time I was in port, you sold me two stiffs."

"Cap'n," the crimp said, shaking his head, "Sometimes the drugs we use to encourage them does 'em in. You know the risks. Wouldn't want them waking up too soon, now would you?"

"Doesn't do to pay for corpses," the captain grumbled.

"Throw in an extra one, no cost to you. Nobody can say Shanghai Kelly's not an honest man."

"An honest thief, you mean."

The two laughed and shook hands. Slocum saw greenbacks changing hands—money paid for him. He had fought on the side of the South during the war because that was his homeland, but like Robert E. Lee, the devotion was to the land and not to the institution of slavery. His father had never owned slaves; John Slocum never had either. Now he was being sold like chattel.

He fought to sit up, then sank back down, not even coming near his goal. While his body still suffered the effects of the drugs given him by Kelly, his brain seemed remarkably clear.

Don't fight it, he thought. *Sit and recover, then get away when no one suspects. Recover from the drug. Recover. Try to . . .*

Slocum passed out.

". . . not like the olden days," Slocum heard a man saying. "I was shanghaied onto the *Reefer*."

"Aw, you're lying. That hell-ship sank twenty years ago."

"God's truth," the first man maintained. "In the mid seventies, it was. The *Reefer* was one of three ships what anchored off the Heads, just outside the Golden Gate. Shanghai Kelly chartered an old paddle-wheel steamer and announced he was celebratin' 'is birthday. Free liquor, all the food you could stuff down your gullet, the son of a bitch even 'inted at free women."

Slocum turned over and sat up, back to the wall. Eight bodies lay like the dead, and the only others showing any sign of life were the two crusty salts talking. Both were sailors sporting lurid tattoos on their brawny forearms, and neither appeared overly upset at the idea of being shanghaied.

"Told everyone in the Barbary Coast to come, he did," said the sailor with the heavy scar on his cheek. "Ninety of us showed. Took two hours of drinkin' his accursed drugged liquor 'fore we passed out. Put us aboard the *Reefer* and the other two ships. That's 'ow I learned my seafarin' skills."

"Didn't anyone notice his paddle wheeler came back empty?" asked Slocum. "Someone must have mentioned missing ninety men."

"The son of a bitch came back an 'ero, don't you know? The *Yankee Blade* had grounded off Point Conception and Kelly rescued 'er crew, he did. Everyone was so glad to see the *Blade*'s crew safe and sound, they never noticed the likes of us missin'."

Slocum shoved himself upright and banged his head on a low ceiling. Walking bent over he examined the tiny room that had become their prison cell.

"Just above the bilge, we are," said the scarred sailor. "No need to be lookin' for escape. Cap'n Goble knows how to watch over his purchases till we're out of sight of land."

Slocum ran his fingers over the iron door barring escape. He didn't have to be told that the lock was more than adequate to hold them in. Even a battering ram would be hard pressed to dent this door. The only other possible exit was in a tiny opening in the ceiling. He twisted around and pressed his face next to the rusty grating. From here he saw out onto the deck.

"Don't go hurtin' yourself none," the second sailor said. "Even if you got that there grate off, you're too burly to get through."

Slocum saw the man was right.

"See any sign that we're gettin' under way?" asked the scarred sailor. "While I could have picked better'n Cap'n Goble, he's nowhere near the tyrant others are."

"That Horvat fella," said the other sailor, shuddering. "I shipped under him. He paid us shit, then put us up in a fancy place ashore when we docked."

"That doesn't sound so bad," said Slocum.

The two looked at him with real pity in their eyes.

"You don't know nothin', do you now, mate? The prices was high, our pay low. The cap'n, he had to bail us out, which put us in his debt. He got another eight-month tour out of us for nothing a'tall but bunk and found."

"And he got a bit of graft from the owner of the boardinghouse where you stayed," said Slocum, un-

derstanding. The ships' captains and the owners of
the waterfront dives were in cahoots, and the sailors
were the ones being robbed blind at every turn. They
worked and died under terrible conditions, and then
the survivors were bilked out of what little they had
been paid.

Slocum sat back down, anger flaring.

"Better get used to the idea, mate. You're in for a
long haul, this time around. Rumors had it Cap'n
Goble wanted to head for the Celestial Kingdom and
try for some of their silks and opium."

"You mean China?"

"None other than. It ain't gonna be so bad, don't
you know? Them little yellow girls know all the tricks,
and they sell themselves cheap. Pennies. For a nickel
they'll screw you cross-eyed and take a week to do
it."

Slocum didn't intend to find out if the sailor was
exaggerating or not. He didn't intend working on any
steamer going to the Orient. But how he was going
to escape eluded him at present. Slocum knew it had
to be done soon or he might as well forget it. In the
middle of the Pacific there'd be no way of ever getting
back to America.

"Engines," said one of the men. "I feel them turning over."

"No," said the other. "That must be the capstan
raising sea anchor. We'll be through the Golden Gate
in another hour."

Slocum got to his feet and peered out the grating.
Men worked on deck now. Through the narrow range
of vision he saw preparations being made for departure. His fingers gripped at the iron grate and he shook
with rage. Damn Kelly!

"They'll be lettin' us out of this stink hole, not that

the crew's quarters are any better," said the scarred sailor. "A breath of salt air will calm you right down."

Slocum didn't calm down. If anything, what he saw increased his excitement. Three men were creeping over the railing and onto the deck—the three men who had followed him from the Cobweb Palace. They spoke in guarded tones too low for him to hear, then they moved out of sight. From the way they acted, they didn't belong aboard this ship. Hope flared in Slocum. The only reason they might be here was to rescue him. It seemed farfetched, and he couldn't give any explanation why they'd bother, especially after he'd roughed one of them up, but it gave him something to hope for.

"Would you two leave if you got out of here?" he asked his fellow prisoners.

"Cap'n Goble's not the best to sail under," said one. "I'd choose better, on my own."

"There's this wee little lass ashore I've not finished with," said the other. "Don't you know I'd be ripped away from her just as things were gettin' interestin'?"

"So you'd leave if you had the chance?"

"We would, but how's the likes of you goin' to get us that chance, eh, mate?"

Slocum said nothing. He sat, straining his ears for the slightest sound out in the corridor. Less than five minutes later he heard guttural cursing and then the sharp report of a pistol being fired in a closed space. Both of his companions leaped to their feet, barely missing the overhead.

"You got friends gettin' us out, do you now?" asked the one.

"Not friends, I don't think," said Slocum. "But we can get off when they open the door. If we do it right."

The door creaked open on rusted hinges. Slocum

helped it along with a foot. The door flew back and smashed into one of the three outside. Slocum let the two sailors out ahead of him. The confusion in the corridor was enough to allow Slocum to get past and start running. The three who had come for him obviously thought all within the tiny cell were still drugged. That anyone had come out startled them. Deep voices shouting at him in Russian echoed down the hall. Slocum didn't stop. Freedom meant more than getting out of the cell; he had to get off the ship— and away from his would-be rescuers.

A bullet came whining after him, bouncing off the walls. One of the Russians jerked the gun the other held and said something. Slocum hoped all that lingo meant they wanted him alive.

He burst out onto the deck and quickly surveyed his surroundings. San Francisco lay a few miles distant, cold water and swift currents separating him from it. Slocum dodged back into the ship's corridors and worked his way up toward the bridge. The captain's cabin probably held all the valuables taken off those being shanghaied, if Kelly hadn't already liberated them before delivering his victims to the ship.

Slocum found the cabin without any problem, but his Colt and money were nowhere to be seen. Slocum searched through a compact desk and found the ship's log, record book, cargo manifests, and other paperwork necessary for running the ship. He cast all these aside. The neat bunk had nothing stored beneath it worth mentioning. The old steamer trunk with hungry green mildew slowly eating away at the leather straps holding it closed contained a dress uniform with gold braid turning green, a few odds and ends, a change of clothes, and two framed pictures of a woman with a small child.

"Where?" Slocum said aloud. "There must be something tucked away in here."

He went to a small chest of drawers and opened the top drawer. Relief washed over him. Inside he found a brace of pistols, old Colt Navys similar to the ones he had carried a few years earlier. Slocum checked, and the percussion caps were in place. He now had some chance of getting away. Thrusting the guns into his belt, he went hunting for the captain.

On deck he heard angry shouts. The two sailors who'd been in the cell with him had been caught. Stout rope tied their hands behind their backs. The captain stood before them, obviously debating whether or not to just throw them, bound as they were, into the harbor.

"But Cap'n," pleaded the one. "We know the work. We weren't tryin' to escape. We was 'untin' for that other fellow, the one what got his friends to come aboard."

That told Slocum a great deal. The three Russians were still loose. And still tracking him down.

Slocum moved to the other side of the ship and peered over to the waterline. A Whitehall boat had been tied to a stanchion; this was the way the three Russians had boarded. And it would be the way Slocum left.

He took advantage of the commotion at the front to make his way to deck level and start over the railing. The cocking of a pistol froze him to the spot.

"We first. Then you," said one of the Russians from the vantage point of a hatchway. He had a revolver pointed directly at Slocum's head. Slocum considered his chances in either just falling over the railing and into the water or trying for one of the Colts he had stuck in his belt. Neither seemed a good bet until a sailor let out a cry and brought several others running.

The Russian turned and fired at the sailor, letting Slocum escape. Slocum had considered getting over the side and into the boat and had discarded it. The sailors would spot him that way and blow him out of the water before he got fifty feet. Boots pounding hard against the planking, he bulled over one sailor and slammed his fist hard into another's stomach.

Slocum ducked into a cabin to catch his breath.

"You would do well not to move, Mr. Slocum."

Standing in the shadows were the other two Russians. Both had their guns trained on him.

"Why did you come aboard? Not to save me."

"But yes, that is why. You make it seem as if we do all this work for nothing, that you like idea of being forced to work and sail to China."

"Can't say that I like it, but can't say I like the idea of being kidnapped by anybody."

One man laughed harshly.

"We must leave soon. There is great uproar over escape."

"I can see why. Shanghai Kelly wouldn't want men coming back to even the score with him."

"You do not understand. Captain of vessel needs crew and does not like idea of being short for three months' cruise to China." The Russian looked out the window. Slocum uneasily watched. The fanatical light burning in the man's eyes told of absolute devotion, to the point of death—but to what cause?

"We go now."

One reached for Slocum's pistols, but the taller of the pair, who had done all the talking, shook his head. "Mr. Slocum will not use these against us. We need firepower to escape ship."

"He is dangerous." The dark cloud coming over the man's face sent chills up Slocum's back. Even as anger formed, the eyes blazed even hotter with fanatical glee. The man actually relished the idea of shooting his way off the ship and would love to see Slocum dead in the bargain.

"Mr. Slocum, we are your only chance off ship. Come with us and we let you keep your guns."

Slocum nodded, intending to get away from his rescuers as soon as he could. They were no better than Captain Goble and his crew of shanghai merchants. And if Slocum's suspicions were right, they might be even worse. Blowing up bemedaled counts with a bomb wasn't the kind of men Slocum courted as friends.

"Ivan, now!" The shorter of the two leaped into the corridor and motioned Ivan and Slocum to hurry.

Gunfire started immediately. The Russian's pistol exploded in his hand as he returned fire, blowing off two fingers, but Slocum had been right about him. The man hardly noticed. Fanaticism burned too harshly for him to take note. Pulling out a knife large enough to kill a deer, the Russian bellowed and rushed the tiny knot of sailors at the entryway. Even though they shot the man repeatedly he kept going, knife slashing, sailors dying.

Ivan shoved Slocum in the other direction. "He will keep them occupied. We go."

Slocum had both Colts out and firing when they emerged from the ship's interior and saw the captain and five of his crew coming from the bow. One pistol emptied, Slocum did a border shift, the pistol in his left hand coming up and over while the one in his right flew straight into his left hand. He only winged one sailor but sent them all scurrying like rats for cover.

"You are good," said Ivan, holding his massive pistol in a meaty hand. He had yet to fire. Slocum wondered if he was worried that the pistol might explode like the other Russian's had.

"Good and ready to leave."

The Russian who had almost caught Slocum climbing over the railing joined them. The trio made their way back to the point where the boat bobbed on its line down below.

"There!" came the shout from the bridge. "There they are. Mow the bastards down!"

The captain's rage knew no bounds. Slocum fired in his general direction, just to drive him back, but the captain stood his ground. With their location known to all aboard ship, Slocum decided that fighting it out toe to toe wasn't the right tactic. During the war he had seen enough action to know that retreats were not cowardly when done for the purpose of living to fight another day. Senseless death didn't make for bravery.

His legs scissored and he was over the rail and falling toward the Whitehall boat. He hit hard, rolled, and almost went over the side when the boat tipped under him. Slocum was pitched in the other direction as Ivan and the other Russian came after.

"Row!" Ivan ordered. From inside his heavy wool coat he produced a knife the brother to the big one the other had used. Ivan drew it across the thick hawser holding the boat to the side of the ship. Strands parted and they cast off.

Bullets plinked into the water around them, giving Slocum all the more reason to put his back into rowing. Ivan fired three rounds and drove the sailors away from the railing long enough for Slocum and the other to row them out of range. All the way the captain shouted obscenities at them.

"Think they'll come after us?" asked Slocum.

"They have no small boat in water. Take too long. Why bother? You cost them much, but might cost more recapturing you. Easier to find another fool to drink in Kelly's saloon."

"That how you tracked me down? Through Kelly?"

"After leaving strange places with bugs all over walls, and striking Yerik, we had difficult time finding your path through maze of city streets."

Ivan's eyes shifted to Yerik, who sat coldly glaring at Slocum. Slocum knew Yerik would kill him the first chance he got for the way he had been humiliated. Slocum's vow to get free of the Russians as soon as possible became even more urgent.

"But," Ivan went on, "we decided you sought information. Docks provide it. So we look and we find. Eventually."

"Did you kill Georgi?" Slocum asked.

"Yerik did."

"What's so important about that jade box that you'd kill for it? It's lovely, it's worth a small fortune, but so many have died over it. Is it worth your life?"

"An odd question, considering your involvement, Mr. Slocum." Ivan's eyes took on the fanatical fire of a true believer. "We will do anything to recover box. It is symbol of our cause, of our oppression!"

They had rowed to within a few hundred yards of a dock at the end of Battery Street. Slocum kept up the rhythm of the stroke but prepared to go over the side at the proper instant. Let them come after him again. Now that he knew his pursuers, it made avoiding them all the easier.

"No, Mr. Slocum," said Ivan in a quiet voice. "You will not swim ashore without us." The heavy revolver aimed squarely at Slocum's chest. "You are our prisoner now and will answer questions of grave importance to our cause."

The unwavering pistol caused Slocum's plan for escape to die. He hoped he wouldn't die along with it.

6

Slocum kept his hands on the oar and rowed until the boat knocked against the pier. Yerik reached over and removed the Colt Navy from Slocum's belt, then gestured for him to climb out.

Slocum stood, tipped the boat with his weight, then dived hard for the dock. The action forced the unmoored boat backward and toward the Bay, and the rocking disturbed Ivan's aim. Slocum slammed hard into the dock and grabbed the splintery wood for dear life. His feet kicked in midair, then he scrambled up and to his feet.

A heavy bullet smashed into the dock and sent wood fragments flying everywhere. A quick glance out at Ivan and Yerik told him the story. They had the boat under control now and Ivan's aim would be better. Slocum ran like all the Creeks in Oklahoma were after him.

"Stop!" cried Ivan, his rage obvious, but by the time the two Russians had gained the dock, Slocum had too big a head start for them to ever overtake him.

He turned off Battery and onto East, slowing his breakneck pace and catching his wind. It had been a busy few days, and getting drugged and shanghaied had worn him out. He held both hands in front of him and noted how they shook. It had been a while since he'd eaten, too. But he didn't have any money, and his Colt had been stolen.

By Shanghai Kelly.

Slocum naturally turned for the saloon and boardinghouse. If he had to use his bare hands to squeeze both money and weapon out of Kelly, he'd do it. The anger at what had been done to him flared brightly enough to keep him going that long.

The saloon was almost deserted at this time of the morning. Slocum paused for a moment before entering, looking to see if Kelly was inside. The sound of the man's voice echoed out into the street. Slocum started in.

A hard poke in the back with a gun barrel staggered him.

"Mr. Slocum, you try even my patience," came Ivan's slow words. "You run from me. I should allow Yerik to ply his skills with you. Before joining our movement, he proved himself able fur trapper. And seal skinner."

Slocum had collapsed to hands and knees, shaking all over in reaction. He was weaker than he'd thought—from lack of food, from mistreatment, even from the aftereffects of the opium he'd been given by Kelly. Looking up he saw Yerik smiling wickedly and drawing his thumb over the edge of a flensing knife. That he wanted to use it on Slocum's hide was obvious.

"I'm weaker than I thought," said Slocum. "No food. Need rest."

"Help him, Yerik. Carefully." Ivan kept back a few paces, the gun in his hand. None of the passersby took notice. Along the docks, in the Barbary Coast, it never paid to meddle in someone else's business, especially when pistols were drawn and pointed.

Slocum wished he'd had strength enough to give

Yerik a good fight. He didn't. The man kept a bone-crushing grip on Slocum's arm as he helped him along.

"Finding you proved too easy this time, Mr. Slocum. Never try for revenge in such obvious ways."

"What way do you suggest? Tossing a bomb under a carriage?"

"Yes!" The word hissed out like water dropped into a campfire. The intensity shook Slocum.

"Social Revolutionaries require obvious symbols," said Yerik.

"Social Revolutionaries?"

Ivan spoke. "Say nothing more, Yerik. We must find Fabergé pianoforte."

Slocum's head had begun to spin around and around until the dizziness forced him to lean heavily on Yerik. The strong Russian had no difficulty in half carrying, half dragging Slocum. Less than ten minutes passed before Ivan unlocked the door to a warehouse down an alley off East Street. Yerik shoved Slocum inside. The man fell heavily to the dirt floor and lay there, dazed.

"He does not pretend. He is giddy from opium."

"I know, Yerik. I watched closely as we came here. This is best time to ask Mr. Slocum our questions. He will thank us for our attentions later, after we have conquered Tsar Alexander."

None of that made sense to Slocum. He clung to simple ideas: Survive. Escape. Get even later.

Yerik kicked him in the side and pain lashed his senses. Slocum moaned and tried to avoid the second kick. He failed. Ribs cracked under the Russian's heavy boot.

"You should not have humiliated Yerik. He never forgets." In a soft voice laced with menace, Ivan added, "None of us does."

"What do you want?" Slocum groaned out from between tightly clenched teeth. Breathing sent liquid fire into his lungs. Yerik had done a good job with just two well-placed kicks.

"Where is Fabergé box?"

"The little jade piano? I don't have it. Don't know." Slocum doubled over in time to take Yerik's boot on his upper arm. While this protected his ribs, it raised a disabling bruise on his biceps.

"You know. Where is it?" Ivan's patience was nearing an end, but Slocum refused to say more than he already had. While he owed Juliana nothing, he wasn't about to turn her over to these men. If he read their intentions right, they were going to try to kill her anyway. Why the jade box—the Fabergé box, as Ivan called it—was so important to them he had no idea. But Juliana deserved it more than these sons of bitches.

"Again, Yerik. Help him remember. Betchkov died in his room trying to get back box. He knows where it is."

Slocum passed out after only three more kicks. He had learned the identity of the man Juliana had killed. But he said nothing about Juliana or the box.

He awoke to darkness. Slocum panicked, thinking they had blinded him, then calmed when he realized a heavy woolen cloth had been tied over his eyes. He tugged at the ropes hog-tying him and found them too tight to give any leeway. Slocum kicked and rolled onto his back, hands pinned beneath his body. This position was too uncomfortable to stay in for long, but he managed to lever himself against a wall and up to a sitting position.

Slocum had to rely on senses other than sight to

tell him about his surroundings. The salt tang to the air told him he was still near the waterfront. The distant slapping of waves against buried pilings added to this. Of people he heard nothing. A sense of space told Slocum he was in a warehouse or some other equally large enclosure. The dank mustiness hinted at disuse, but of that he wasn't so sure. He doubted he had been moved from the warehouse they had originally taken him to.

His Russian captors had done well in making sure he didn't meddle in their affairs.

Anger built inside him as he thought not only of Ivan and Yerik but of Shanghai Kelly. There'd be a day of reckoning. Soon. But first things first. Slocum began rubbing his head against the rough-planked wall until he hooked a splinter on the cloth. He dropped low and pulled the blindfold away.

Again he worried that he had gone blind. He saw nothing at first in the darkness. Dim outlines began forming and confirmed his suspicions that he was in a warehouse. Dirty windows high on one wall looked out into a moonlit night. Slocum worked his way to his feet, using the rough wall as a support, and hopped about looking for an edge sharp enough to cut through his ropes. Light-headedness worked against him. He had been beaten and drugged and kidnapped and too many other things to remember clearly, and it all took its toll on him now.

But Slocum not only didn't give up, he used the anger he felt toward all who had used him so badly to his own advantage. He hopped and fell forward, twisting to land beside a pile of broken glass. Working clumsily he cut through the ropes binding him like a calf at spring branding, then used the largest shard to slash the ropes on his ankles.

"Now," he said softly. "Things will be different now."

He rubbed the blood back into his hands and went looking for an exit. He found one barred door, but an argument going on across the warehouse floor drew Slocum's full attention. He turned his steps in that direction and, as if stalking game in the forest, he hunted.

Yerik, Ivan, and four other Russians sat in a tight circle around a small fire. The dancing light cast evil shadows on their faces, turning them into things less than human. While Yerik and Ivan talked rapidly in Russian, the others spoke English.

Ivan quickly shifted languages, saying to one of the men, "You are certain she will be at funeral?"

"No question of it," the man said solemnly. "She will be eliminated as she emerges from the building."

"She might have Fabergé box," protested Ivan. "To kill her is to remove all chance of finding it."

"Box is important," agreed Yerik, "but Countess Rumyantsova's death is more important to cause."

"I care little for such deaths. The value of the box transcends monetary considerations," said another man around the tiny fire. Slocum squinted at him. His words came out cultured, even educated. When he bent forward to warm his hands and take some of the San Francisco Bay chill out of his joints, Slocum saw that he was richly dressed and his hands hadn't seen even a day's hard work. "While the money is needed for our cause," he went on, "the symbol of that box is much greater. It shows the peasants how their precious tsar squanders Mother Russia's wealth!"

The words burned with fiery fanaticism. Slocum wasn't as interested in that as he was in talk of assassinating this Countess Rumyantsova. He had a gut feeling he knew the countess's first name.

"Cowboy knows where box is. Killing countess is not going to prevent recovering Fabergé box." Yerik cleaned his fingernails with the flensing knife, using deft, quick movements. "Let me ask questions of him. I will discover where box is hidden."

"We work at cross-purposes," said the educated man. "We need to narrow our activities and concentrate on only one or two if we are to succeed. This captive of yours—kill him. Kill the countess also, if that pleases you. But we must recover the pianoforte miniature, if possible, and, even more important, protect the other Fabergé pieces."

"The egg," said another man. "Lovely piece of work that egg."

"Fabergé egg," said Ivan, nodding. "We will have it out of the city and on its way to the rancho soon."

Slocum blinked in surprise at hearing a Spanish word so oddly spoken by the Russian.

"Other items, too," added Yerik. "All will be safe until need arises for their use."

"Good," said the educated man, rising. "Take care of it. You have done well so far, except in the matter of letting the pianoforte miniature slip from our grasp."

"Sailors are dead," said Yerik with some satisfaction.

"We did not even know Georgi and Stephan knew of the items," said Ivan.

"No matter. This is all history now. Do not repeat such mistakes in the future. Get the jade box and let's get on with our individual assignments."

"To revolution!" cried Ivan.

Yerik and the others joined in for a second chorus.

Slocum used the noise to cover his quick steps away and back to the barred door. He looked around, knowing he had only a few minutes before Yerik came to kill him. Slocum decided flight now was better than taking on the knife-wielding Russian. While the light-headedness had passed, Slocum didn't want to chance a fight with someone rested and well fed—and armed.

He smiled when he saw a stack of boxes stairstepping their way up the side of the warehouse. Slocum clambered up on one after another until he reached the top. The pile of crates teetered precariously, but he wasn't going to stay on them long. He judged the distance to the dirty-paned window and jumped.

Slocum grunted as his fingers closed on the dusty window ledge. He pulled himself up and used his shoulder to push open the window. Its rusty hinges protested enough to make a noise Slocum thought would awaken the dead. He paused, listened hard, and decided Yerik hadn't heard. Slocum pushed on through the window, his body snaking through until he dangled outside. Kicking away from the wall, he dropped the fifteen feet and landed hard enough to rattle his teeth.

His entire body ached from the beating he'd gotten at Yerik's hand, and giddiness crept up on him once more. Slocum fought it down and started walking, the chill breeze blowing off the Bay giving him a clearer head even as it made him shiver.

He hadn't done too well in the past few days. He'd been shanghaied, lost his money and gun, been done out of the jade box—the Fabergé box, whatever that meant—and had been beaten up by the Russians plotting political assassinations as calmly as he might decide whether he wanted steak or bacon for breakfast.

The thought of food made his mouth water. His belly rumbling like a mountain storm, Slocum picked up the pace as he headed for Shanghai Kelly's. Soon he would have his fill of food—and revenge.

He had lain half asleep most of the night watching the back door of Kelly's Saloon and Boardinghouse. A few people had come and gone, but not Kelly. Slocum struggled to his feet and moved forward to peer in a back window. The scene hadn't changed much from the last time he had looked. Kelly and five others were playing poker, huge piles of chips and greenbacks on the table.

"He's using my money," Slocum said to himself. The anger drove away the mind-dulling clouds of fatigue threatening to close around him. He reached down and picked up a piece of spar about the thickness of his wrist. Slocum hefted it and decided this made as good a weapon as he was likely to find.

Another twenty minutes brought the faint pinks and yellows of dawn to the sky over the Bay—and the end of the poker game. By ones and twos the players filed out the back door of Kelly's, until only Kelly himself sat at the table counting his considerable winnings.

"It's easy to win with a shaved deck," Slocum said from the doorway.

Kelly whirled around, his hand already reaching for a derringer in a cuff holster. But Slocum hadn't been caught unawares. The thick spar crashed into Kelly's wrist. The dull crunching told of broken bones. The howl of pain told of the agony given by those broken bones.

"Who are you?" Kelly demanded. He squinted so

hard his eyes all but vanished into pits of gristle. "You don't know who I am, bucko, or you'd never try to rob me."

"That, Mr. Kelly, is not so. I know exactly who you are."

Kelly tried to stand. Slocum used the spar on the man's kneecap. Another crunch and Kelly crashed face forward to the floor, unable to break his fall because of the ruined wrist. Slocum added another love tap to keep the saloon owner and shanghaier flat.

"You don't recognize me," Slocum said, his tone sarcastic. "You never remember those you send out to work and maybe die, do you? Makes it easier to sleep at night."

"Look, mister, you got the wrong man." Kelly spoke through clenched teeth. All the while he struggled to reach his derringer. Slocum let him awkwardly pull it out before he struck again with the spar. Both of Kelly's wrists were broken now.

"I got the right man. Only one bushwhacking son of a bitch like you I know of. Might be others, but the others didn't drug me and sell me for twenty dollars to be a sailor."

"Nothin' wrong with being a seaman, bucko," Kelly said, but his voice was taking on shriller tones. He now feared for his life. Once again Slocum anticipated the man's move. The spar dropped down and rested against Kelly's lips. The threat was obvious: Try to call out for help and have all the teeth shoved down his throat.

Slocum picked up the derringer.

"Where's my pistol?" he asked. "Colt Peacemaker."

"Don't have it. Don't know," Kelly muttered.

Slocum cocked the derringer and aimed it directly

between Kelly's frightened eyes. The temptation to pull the trigger was almost greater than Slocum could resist. But he did.

"My pistol," he repeated. "Where?"

Kelly's eyes darted toward a box at the far corner of the room. Never letting the muzzle of the small gun stray from its target, Slocum crossed the room and began poking around in the box Kelly had inadvertently indicated. Slocum smiled. On top lay his .44–.40, his gunbelt, and a half dozen other revolvers. Slocum hastily buckled on his gun and felt safer than he had in days.

"From the looks of all this hardware, you've been busy, Mr. Kelly." Slocum helped himself to the winnings off the table, taking the greenbacks and leaving the chips. He didn't intend returning here.

"You're dead meat, you bastard," said Kelly. "No man does this to me. No one!"

Slocum's lips curled into a tiny smile. "You're right, Mr. Kelly. I have been treating you poorly. Here, let me help you." Slocum reached into Kelly's coat pocket and found the opium-laden cigars. He bit off one end and lit the cigar, puffing lightly enough to get the smoke going. "Here. Enjoy one of your own special Chinese cigars."

Kelly's eyes widened in fear. Pain etched his face, but panic soon outraced it.

"Smoke or I'll blow your damned brains all over the floor." Slocum cocked his Colt and stuck it into Kelly's left ear.

"Wrists are broken," Kelly grated out. "Can't hold it."

"I'll help you. Just to show you what a kindhearted fellow I can be." Slocum made sure that Kelly sucked in the noxious fumes. By the time the saloon owner had reduced the cigar to a one-inch butt and a pile of ash, he lay in a drugged stupor on the floor.

Slocum looked around the small back room, poking into nooks and crannies, and found the watch his brother Robert had had on him at Gettysburg when he was killed. Slocum returned it to its usual resting place in his vest pocket. He found a few more greenbacks and a stack of twenty-dollar gold pieces—all recently taken off Kelly's victims.

"Hey, Mr. Kelly, when ya want to ship these poor sonsabitches?" came the shout from the saloon itself.

"Right away," Slocum answered, hoping he muffled his voice enough to pass for Kelly. "Got one more. In the back room."

"That one for Cap'n Goble?"

"That he is," said Slocum, smiling broadly. He went to Kelly and stripped off the man's coat, vest, and shirt. He found a burlap bag and tied it over the man's head. The boots and trousers came off, as did the flashy rings Shanghai Kelly wore. Slocum had some problem with this because the fingers had swollen up, but he managed. Kelly was past caring about a little discomfort. His own opium smoke had sent him to a land free of pain and sorrow.

Slocum slipped out the back way and watched as two burly men entered. One pointed to the body on the floor. The other opened a trapdoor in the floor. They dropped Kelly down it, to a boat moored under the dock, and never once checked to see who their victim might be. This was routine for them, a shanghai kidnapping that was old hat.

Slocum laughed aloud after the pair had slammed the trapdoor. When Kelly awoke, he'd be on a steamer plowing through the Pacific, heading for the Orient.

Slocum patted the roll of bills he had stuffed into his shirt pocket.

"Breakfast, at Mr. Shanghai Kelly's expense," he said. "Steak *and* bacon."

After a double portion of everything, Slocum's belly stopped its complaining. Hot black coffee kept him from dozing off and got him out of the small café and looking up and down the street with clear eyes. A street urchin selling papers caught his attention.

"See what's happenin' in San Francisco," the boy called out in a loud voice. "Gitcher *Examiner* here!"

Slocum tossed the boy a nickel and quickly scanned the paper. It took less than a minute to find the obituary of Count Borov and the information Slocum needed. He oriented himself, then headed off for High Street and the funeral parlor where the count's body would lie in state until being packed up and prepared for the trip back to Russia.

It was a little past nine when Slocum found the funeral home. Several expensive carriages had been parked to the side, their drivers idly passing a small flask around to kill the time. Slocum surveyed the street and saw nothing out of the ordinary. From inside the small building he heard a song welling up. He strained to recognize it and decided the words were in Russian.

He settled down to wait awhile and see what happened.

By nine-thirty the Russian Orthodox ceremony inside had run its course and the nobles decked out in medals and jeweled sashes were leaving the funeral parlor. Slocum came to his feet. A tenseness in the air grew until he wanted to scream.

Juliana emerged from the front door, a Russian army officer at her elbow. Even from this distance Slocum saw she'd been crying. He started across the street.

The pounding of hooves and the clatter of carriage wheels on the cobblestones added speed to his step. He barely avoided being run down by the driver.

"Juliana, look out!" he called. Shots rang out. The Russian nobles scattered, taking cover. The young officer beside Juliana sank to his knees, a startled expression on his face. He fell forward without saying a word.

The carriage wheeled about. Inside, Slocum saw Yerik and another of the Social Revolutionaries. Their driver whipped the horses, and the carriage sped back in the direction it had come. Slocum didn't bother trying to draw his Colt and fire. He ran as if the hounds of hell were on his heels. He'd seen what Yerik had held in his hand.

"John?" the lovely, dark-haired woman asked. "I . . ."

He didn't take time to explain. Still running at top speed, Slocum scooped up the woman. She struggled as one arm circled her waist and the other flung open the funeral parlor door.

"Stop it!" Juliana cried.

He drove forward, falling on top of her. They slid a few feet on the highly polished marble floor. Then the entire front of the building exploded inward.

7

The world blasted apart on top of Slocum's head. The cascade of plaster and brick after the explosion was almost as bad. He kept his head down, his arms and body protecting Juliana. Only when the dust began to settle did he get up onto his knees and look at the woman.

Juliana lay still on the floor, now tattered and dirty in her once-regal gown.

Slocum's heart missed a beat when he thought the woman might be dead. He reached down and lightly shook her.

"Juliana? Are you all right?" He rolled her onto her back. A tiny cut had opened above her eye and was bleeding, but it was minor and would obviously cause more damage to a fancy hairdo than to her health. He placed one finger onto the side of her swanlike throat and found the slow pulse there. She was alive.

Blue eyes flickered open and focused on him. "John? What happened? I saw you, then the shots and . . ."

"Come on, get up," Slocum said, helping her to unsteady feet. He wasn't all that sure of his own step. It had been a long time since he'd gotten a good night's sleep, and the effects of the strong black coffee he'd drunk for breakfast had begun to wear off.

"The guard?" she asked. "Is he dead?"

"Believe so," said Slocum, looking toward the back of the funeral parlor. Count Borov's coffin had been closed and still stood on a small bier at the end of the room. A few flowers had been stuffed into vases; the explosion and heat wave following it had destroyed the fragile buds and littered the floor with multicolored petals.

Juliana started toward the front, where the blast had destroyed the door. Slocum firmly took her by the arm and guided her away.

"Not that way. They might still be waiting. They wanted to kill you, just as they did the count."

"What? Who?" Juliana asked. But Slocum read her perfectly now, as if her every thought was spelled out for him. The shock of the bombing had passed and she was in full possession of her senses. The dark-haired woman simply didn't want to give anything away.

"I'll hand it to you," he said. "You sure play your cards close to your chest." Slocum smiled and looked at the swell of her breasts pressing into the dirtied velvet of her expensive gown. "And I don't blame you much either."

"You know?" she asked.

"About the Social Revolutionaries? Some. They kidnapped me—after rescuing me."

"I am sorry, John. Your involvement is not something I sought out. You should never had even seen the jade box."

"The Fabergé box?"

Her plucked eyebrows rose. "You know a great deal about this matter, then."

"Enough to know they want you dead. Me, too." He pulled her along behind him like a child's captive balloon. Juliana went without resisting. The back door from the funeral parlor opened into one of the numerous alleyways dotting San Francisco. Slocum started uphill, going toward the Pacific Ocean. He had no clear idea where to hide, but getting away from the funeral parlor had to be at least as good an idea as any he'd had in a long, long time.

"Wait, John. Let's go to my house. It is not too far from here."

"Do they know about it? Ivan and Yerik and the other Social Revolutionaries?"

"Their names are unknown to me, but of course I do know of the Social Revolutionaries," she said with great loathing. "They are the cause of much of Russia's problems today."

"Your house. Do they know where it is?" Slocum repeated. He didn't want a long lecture on Russian politics. He wanted somewhere to clean up, to rest, to get away from men trying to kill him.

"I doubt it. The house was leased under another name by a sympathizer who has graciously allowed me to use it while in this city. It is near Russian Hill."

"Figures," he said. Slocum didn't want to stay on the streets, not with a carriage laden with bomb-throwing assassins still cruising around. He summoned a passing carriage and let Juliana give the directions. He leaned back and fought the urge to close his eyes. Slocum kept one hand resting on the butt of his Colt. He knew he might have to use it on a second's notice.

"All will be well, John. Trust me," Juliana said.

"Trust you?" His laugh came out harsher than he intended, but he didn't apologize. "You stole what rightly belonged to me. I won that jade box in a fair poker game. One of the few in all San Francisco, I'd reckon."

"The box was not the sailor's to lose. He stole it."

"Looks like everyone's stolen it. You stole it off me."

Juliana smiled, and a wicked twinkle came to her eyes. "You had no complaints about all that went before, did you?" Her hand rested lightly on his arm, warm, inviting. "You must not carry a grudge for this because you saved my life."

"Wasn't worth the price of the box," he complained.

Juliana stiffened and stared straight ahead, not answering.

"Need to know what's going on," Slocum said. But they both knew he would have rescued her even if she hadn't possessed the details of this circle of theft and killing.

"Driver!" Juliana called out. "Here."

Slocum paid the driver and they watched the carriage rattle off down a steep hill. Slocum was glad they hadn't walked all the way. He would have been dead on his feet by the time they scaled this miniature mountain in the middle of the city.

"Down there," she said, taking a winding path leading back down the side of the hill. "A precaution. If we were followed, I did not want to lead them directly to my house."

Slocum had kept a sharp eye out. They hadn't been trailed, but he approved of Juliana's caution. Carelessness had caused him enough grief already.

The house was more modest than he would have thought in this highfalutin neighborhood. Almost a cottage, it was set in the middle of a well-tended garden and had walls covered in climbing smelly bougainvillea already trying to burst into bloom. San Francisco weather changed little from winter to summer, but the plants knew when to respond, and spring was only a few short months away. Slocum wished he'd be long gone by the time those red blooms appeared, but Oregon and the string of horses he intended to run seemed farther away than ever.

"Come in, please," Juliana said. Slocum entered and closed the door behind him. "Sit down. I think there might still be some coffee left in the pot. Heat it up while I change." A wry expression crossed Juliana's face as she looked down at her ruined gown. She smiled and turned, but Slocum gripped her arm and pulled her back.

She started to protest, but Slocum quieted her with a kiss. The woman melted slowly into the circle of his arms, and the kiss became more passionate. Soon Slocum's heart was trip-hammering and he felt the rising tides within his loins that wouldn't be denied.

"You wanted out of the dress," he said. "Let me help you."

"I'd like that," Juliana said in a little-girl voice. She took a half step back and stood, arms at her sides, waiting. The flushed expression told Slocum she was as eager as he was.

He fumbled a little at the unfamiliar fasteners on the side of her dress. Tiny pearl buttons were intricately fashioned and woven through the fabric, but once he got the hang of it, the dress fell away, exposing Juliana to the waist.

Her unfettered breasts swung freely, high and firm and capped with coppery nipples. Slocum kissed the woman's lush red lips again, then worked his way along the line of her jaw, to the hollow of her throat, lower.

"Oh, John, this feels so nice," she said. He attended

to the canyon between her breasts, kissing and relishing the feel of her gently swaying body on either side of his head.

"Have you any idea who I am?" she asked.

"Pretty, damn pretty," he said. "And all woman." He didn't neglect either breast, his mouth moving, stimulating, arousing both of them even more than they already were.

"I am the Countess Juliana Rumyantsova, member of the Court of St. Petersburg." She shivered delicately when he began working farther down her body, fingers stroking and lips caressing. "I am a confidante of Tsar Alexander and a lady-in-waiting to Tsarina Marie Feodorovna. In Russia I am very powerful."

"In San Francisco you're the loveliest woman of them all."

Slocum found the fasteners for Juliana's skirt. The heavy velvet dropped to the floor. She stepped out of it. Slocum wasted no time getting her out of the frilly undergarments she wore. The sight of the woman's milk-white skin, the dark patch between her slender thighs, and the breasts bobbing about, nipples erect with passion, produced a painful response at Slocum's crotch.

"Let me," Juliana said. "It is only fitting."

She unfastened his gunbelt and dropped it onto a chair. His shirt and trousers quickly followed. Soon enough they both stood buck naked and staring at one another.

"I must be a sorry sight," Slocum said. He ached all over like a son of a bitch, he'd picked up more than his share of cuts and bruises, and he badly needed a bath.

Juliana reached out and took his hard length in her hand. Fingers gently closed and tugged him closer.

"You are exciting," she said softly. They kissed again, slowly moving toward the bedroom.

Juliana writhed in joy as the satin comforter on the bed stroked over her skin. Slocum loved the feel of the woman more than anything else, though. His hands moved slowly over the mounds of her tits, down to the sleek plain of her gently heaving belly, even lower.

"Oh, yes, John, yes!" she gasped as his middle finger invaded her most intimate territory. Hips hunching up off the bed began to grind around and around until his hand was drenched with her juices. "So nice," she sobbed out. "But I want more. I want you. I want this!"

Her thighs parted in wanton invitation. Slocum didn't have to be asked twice. He was already hurting from the intensity of his arousal. The man grunted when fingers drummed along his iron-hard cock and pulled him straight for the carnal target they both sought to have filled.

Slocum stopped for a moment, holding himself on his hands and looking down into the woman's face. A soft pink flush had risen to her shoulders and neck, making her even lovelier than ever before. Her eyes were closed, and the delicately formed face now wore a mask of stark pleasure.

He couldn't hold himself back any longer—and there was no need to. He slipped forward, touched the liquid paradise promised him, sank deeply into the woman's center. Slocum paused and bent down to kiss those lips so invitingly parted for him. Their tongues began moving to and fro in the exact rhythm of their hips, adding to their excitement. The way her hard nipples poked into his chest made the man wonder if she would puncture him with the points.

He couldn't think of anything he'd like more.

They had started at a fever pitch, then slowed and held one another, still locked together at their groins. The tides of passion rose again, and Slocum wasn't able to restrain himself, to prolong this wondrous screwing.

"John, yes, oh, yes, so good, so good," Juliana moaned out. He knew she barely knew what she was saying, her ecstasy was at such a level. Slocum hardly knew what he muttered himself as they swung into a quicker movement, a more animal coupling. They strove together in fluid delight until both burst and clung to one another as their bodies erupted in wild release.

"You're actually worth saving," Slocum said, lying beside the woman on the satin comforter. His hands moved restlessly over her breasts, her belly, her curving asscheeks.

"I am glad you think so," Juliana said. "If it had not been for you, I would have died in the explosion. My bodyguards were looking for the Fabergé egg."

"Tell me what's going on? You have bodyguards? It's obvious you need them, but most folks in this country don't need them. Most ordinary folks."

"I told you I am Countess Rumyantsova. Russian nobility."

"You speak good English. Not like Ivan and the others."

Juliana laughed, and the sound was more than music. "I have spent little time growing up in Russia. I was born just outside of Moscow, raised and educated in Paris and London, traveled widely in America, and only upon Tsar Alexander's assumption of the throne and Tsarina Marie Feodorovna's need for a sophisticated lady-in-waiting have I been much in St. Petersburg."

"How come your bodyguard is somewhere else. I'd think this would be a job no man would shirk." Slocum's finger lightly probed between the woman's thighs. She rolled over on the bed and faced him, her own hands working through the hair on his chest and raising tiny spires.

"They and Prince Golitsyn seek out the Social Revolutionaries."

"A prince, huh? And you're a countess. Is this Tsar Alexander sending all his royalty to San Francisco?"

"He would send the entire army, if that would accomplish his purpose," Juliana said. A grim note crept into her tone. Slocum said nothing. Simply lying next to the woman was enough for now.

"The Social Revolutionaries," she went on, "had committed another terrible crime. They assassinated Tsar Alexander's father in March 1881. A bomb. That is their favorite weapon of terror."

"Works," observed Slocum. "Sure scared the bejesus out of me."

Bright blue eyes studied his face—the strong lines, the firm jaw, and the unwavering gaze. "Nothing frightens you, my hero," she said.

Slocum had to smile wanly at that. She didn't know what terrified him, the dreams—nightmares—of his days with Quantrill, the mutilations and deaths he saw in the war, the evil visited upon the South by the carpetbaggers. Many things scared him shitless, but maybe Juliana was right about one thing. He did show true courage by living with the fear rather than running from it. That made for bravery, and Slocum had to count himself as brave. No matter what, John Slocum did not turn tail and run.

"Those pig-dogs have done more than kill Tsar Alexander's father. Tsar Alexander lives almost like a monk, eating only gruel and living in Gatchina Park rather than in the Winter Palace."

"But there's something that sets him aside," said Slocum, seeing the way Juliana's trail of thought ran.

"The Fabergé egg. The miniatures."

"What's this Fabergé?"

"Not 'what,' John my love, 'who.' Carl Fabergé is an artisan without peer. He crafts the most delicate miniatures, the finest of picture frames, the most ornate and elaborate of clocks and other mechanisms— and all from gold and precious gems."

"The jade box was pretty good work," Slocum agreed.

"Without equal anywhere in the world," corrected Juliana. "But the Social Revolutionaries do not look at how Tsar Alexander lives, they see only the Fabergé masterpieces he buys. This is Alexander's one weakness—pleasing his wife."

"Tsarina Marie Feodorovna?"

"She is European and accustomed to the finest of everything, spending freely. Tsar Alexander lives like a soldier in the field; she, like a true queen."

"These Fabergé trinkets don't strike me as being something a soldier would fancy."

"Ah, John, there is the tsar's one indulgence. Not the Fabergé pieces, but his wife. The egg was the product of close work between Carl Fabergé and Tsar Alexander. It is exquisite, from all accounts."

"The Social Revolutionaries have stolen it?"

"Yes." Juliana's voice turned hard. "They seek to embarrass the tsar with such flagrant waste of gold from the Russian treasury, to show the peasants how the tsar exploits them while they starve. But it is a minor thing for the ruler of such a huge country to want to give his wife the *frisson* of pleasure when she opens her present on Easter morning. Is it so wrong to give the one you deeply love something that will be remembered long after?"

"This Fabergé egg is an Easter present," Slocum said, the pieces fitting together, "and the Social Revolutionaries have stolen it. You were sent—you and Prince Golitsyn and Count Borov, to recover it. But why did the Social Revolutionaries bring it to San Francisco?"

"This is one of the few places on earth where they have sympathizers."

"You said your name was Rumyantsova?"

"You recognize it," Juliana said. "Yes, my great-uncle founded Port Rumyantsov for the Russian-American Company in 1812."

"Port Rumyantsov," mused Slocum. "Fort Ross? Out near Bodega Bay?"

"Some twenty miles to the north. He, ninety-five Russians, and eighty Aleuts settled there in what they called Slavyansk, a redwood fort that was to be the basis of future Russian settlement in California."

"Never worked out?"

"The grain crops were better than in Mother Russia, but the distance and support required by the colony were too great for true success. In 1850 the colony was officially abandoned."

"There are still Russians there, though," said Slocum. "They support these Social Revolutionaries? Why? What does politics in Russia have to do with them. They're all Americans now."

"The roots run deeply, John," Juliana said. She heaved a reluctant sigh and pushed away from him, sitting up and pulling the sheets about her body. He didn't want to let her go.

"They still believe Russia will assert herself and

form a new, stronger colony. Tsar Alexander is against this. There are troubles enough at home without attempting expansion of a worldwide empire." Juliana made a wry face. "Russia for the Russians, Tsar Alexander says. And he means this with all his heart and soul."

Juliana stood and went to her clothes closet. Slocum lay back on the bed and enjoyed the movement of her limbs, the white flash of her thighs, the occasional glimpse of the paradise between her legs. Juliana selected garments and dressed plainly enough— for a Russian countess. She looked back at Slocum on the bed and smiled. Juliana reached into the wardrobe.

"This is for my savior, my hero. Stand," she ordered, the bite of command in her voice. Slocum stood, still naked.

"I present you with the order of St. George for service to the Tsar and Tsarina of Imperial Russia." Juliana draped the ribbon sash over Slocum's left shoulder and pulled it around to fasten it at his left hip. A huge sunburst of emerald- and ruby-encrusted gold hung in the center of the purple ribbon. She kissed him on the cheek.

"That's all I get?" he asked. He yelped when she reached down and took him in hand. Juliana dropped to her knees and kissed his slowly rising manhood, then hastily abandoned it.

"You must do more brave acts to win another medal," she said.

"Isn't rising from the dead enough show of courage? Having you counting coup like that with your lips is getting me all hot and bothered again."

Juliana laughed and shook her head. "There is much

I need to do. And you, for all your eagerness, are pale and drawn. Rest, my hero. When Prince Golitsyn returns, we will discuss this further. I think you will like Dmitri."

The way Juliana spoke the Russian prince's name convinced Slocum he wouldn't cotton to the man at all.

"Here, put on this dressing gown. You look so cold with nothing on." She reached back into the wardrobe and pulled out a long silk robe, obviously belonging to a man. Slocum felt himself tightening a mite. He wondered if this belonged to Dmitri.

Juliana spun away and went into the other room. He heaved a deep sigh, put on the robe, and lay back down on the bed. It wasn't anything to get mad over. She wasn't any virgin. Hell, he was glad of that. Juliana was all woman, with a woman's knowledge and desires. She hadn't got that way being chaste.

But Slocum still didn't think he'd like Dmitri Golitsyn.

He lay back on the bed, eyes closed, listening to the woman going about her chores out in the kitchen. For all her royal upbringing, Juliana Rumyantsova didn't show any concern over getting her hands dirty with work. He heard her laying the wood in the stove and lighting it. The clang of a metal coffeepot as Juliana placed it on the top. Slocum drifted further and further into sleep.

All Juliana had told him made sense. The maze he had wandered through now straightened out, and the journey's end was in sight. He'd have to tell her what he had overheard Ivan and Yerik saying about riding to Bodega Bay and then farther north to Fort Ross.

Sympathizers with the Social Revolutionaries, Juliana had said. Yes, he'd definitely have to tell her. Retrieve the tsar's Easter egg.

Slocum fell into a heavy sleep.

He had no idea how long he had slept when a loud crashing sound awoke him. Sitting bolt upright, he called out, "Juliana, what's wrong?"

He heard muffled cries from the other room. Slocum thought he must be having a nightmare. New sounds of struggle came, and the crash of china breaking on the floor. He jumped from the bed, the silk robe clinging to his legs. He burst into the room and took it all in. Like a daguerreotype, everything burned permanently into his mind.

Juliana, hands tied behind her back and a gag stuffed into her mouth. Ivan behind her. Yerik with his flensing knife. Two others, with revolvers in hand. The chair with his clothes draped over it. His Colt lying on top of his clothes.

Slocum erupted like a colt away from a branding iron, intent on reaching his pistol.

The Russian standing closest to Slocum already had his pistol leveled. Slocum saw his finger drawing back on the trigger, turning white with pressure, lifting the muzzle of the gun up ever so slightly with strain. He saw Juliana's blue eyes go wide. He heard the shot. He felt the bullet strike.

Arms flailing, Slocum pitched back into the bedroom, the heavy bullet hitting square in the middle of his chest.

8

Pain welled up within Slocum's chest, forcing him back to life. The man tried to lift his arms, to move his body, to even open his eyes. The pain that brought him consciousness refused to let him move. It didn't seem fair.

Slocum blinked hard and looked straight ahead. All he saw was whitewashed plaster. For a few seconds this made no sense to him, then he figured out that he was lying stretched out on his back staring up at Juliana's ceiling.

"Juliana!" he called.

The man winced as if some demented fiend had rammed a red-hot poker into his chest, but the thought of the Russian countess being the captive of Ivan—Yerik!—overcame the agony. Juliana Rumyantsova was nowhere to be seen in the small cottage. Slocum tried to remember exacctly what had happened. The Social Revolutionaries in the room remained as clear to him as the instant he walked in on them. His clothes and Colt hadn't been touched. Slocum struggled to his feet and staggered to the chair, using it for support.

He pulled forth his Peacemaker and held the heavy pistol in a shaky hand. Strength returned slowly. He could handle anything that came his way now.

"Shot," he said suddenly. "The bastard shot me."

Looking down, he saw a neat hole in the front of

the rumpled silk dressing gown he wore. Gingerly, he pulled it away to look at his chest. Slocum expected to see a gaping hole the size of his thumb. Instead he uncovered the gaudy gold medallion Juliana had draped over his shoulder. The half-dozen precious stones had popped out of their setting—and one had been struck squarely by the bullet, shattering it. The impact of the slow-moving, large-caliber bullet had been absorbed by the jewel and the heavy gold disk. The only damage Slocum had taken was a huge bruise already turning vivid green and purple.

"Now I know what good these things are," he said, pulling off the ribbon holding the medallion. He shucked off the robe and began dressing. By the time he pulled on his boots, Slocum felt almost normal. Almost. Tiredness still caused his eyelids to droop, and the pain in his chest made him wonder if a rib or two had cracked, but other than this he was in good shape.

And madder than a wet hen.

"You won't keep her," he said. "Wherever you murderous sons of bitches are, I'll find you." He remembered Juliana's yielding flesh next to his, the feel of her surrounding him as they made love, the heat of her breath on his skin, the intelligence and determination she had shown in getting back Tsar Alexander's trinket.

Slocum didn't care squat about the Fabergé egg, but he wanted Juliana Rumyantsova freed from the bomb-throwing assassins.

He prowled around the cottage, looking for some hint as to where they might have taken her. He doubted they would return to the warehouse on the docks. That was one hideout already discovered. But where? Could he possibly find Juliana simply by knocking on every door in San Francisco? Slocum shook his head when he realized that he'd need a powerful lot of luck to ever track her down in a city this size.

Slocum wished they were out in the forests. There he knew how to find spoor, to detect the crushed grass and bent twigs and listen to the way the animals responded. There he was the hunter and knew how to find his prey. Here, in urban San Francisco, he might be the hunter, but where would his prey hide?

Slocum had no idea.

He sank into the chair and tried to figure out what to do. The key to this lock lay in being smarter than the Social Revolutionaries, or using information about them that they didn't know he had. Ivan had mentioned Fort Ross, but Slocum didn't think they would take Juliana there. It was several days' ride up the coast. What they wanted from her was hidden in San Francisco. They wanted the return of the jade Fabergé miniature pianoforte.

And her death.

"How do I find her?" Slocum asked himself over and over. No easy answer came, yet he felt he almost had it time and again. Then Slocum sat back in the chair and relaxed, smiling. "The man with Ivan and Yerik. The one who sounded like he had some book learning."

It wasn't much, but Slocum had an idea where to find the man. He heaved himself up, gently rubbed the sore spot in the center of his chest, and left the cottage nestled on the side of Russian Hill. He had a score to settle with another Russian.

The jewelry store was located on the southern slope of Telegraph Hill. The neighborhood wasn't much to Slocum's liking, nor were the dozen or so Russians

loitering around the front of the store, winking at
women who chanced to pass by, making lewd com-
ments among themselves, and occasionally passing a
bottle of clear liquor around for each to take a swig.
He had seen the educated revolutionary—if he was
the owner of the store, his name was Metchnikovitch—enter and stay inside most of the day. Slocum
wanted to amble by, peer into the tiny front window,
and see what he could see, but the man knew better
than to try.

Yerik was one of those lounging around outside.
The instant he spotted Slocum, all hell would break
loose.

The jewelry store occupied the ground floor of a
four-story wood structure. Slocum saw no sign of
habitation on the upper two levels, though someone
frequently brushed against the brown chintz curtains
in the back window on the second floor. Whoever it
was, Slocum was sure it wasn't Juliana.

He walked down the block, around the corner, up
Telegraph Hill a ways, then returned to a vantage point
several doors down the street from the jewelry store.
It'd take the entire First Virginia Brigade to storm that
place, Slocum figured.

He was fresh out of firepower like that.

What made the waiting all the worse was that he
had no idea if Juliana were even inside the building.
When dusk began to settle, with its cold, blustery
chill, Slocum watched the oil lamps on the second
floor being lit. Three rooms; at least three men.
Metchnikovitch closed the shop, barred the door, and
walked around to the side and spoke with Yerik and
three others for a while. The five men turned and
walked past where Slocum clung to the shadowy depths
of an alley.

As they passed, he heard Metchnikovitch saying, "It is foolish to keep her. So what if she knows the location of the box?"

"Ivan wants box," said Yerik. "It is important to cause."

"This is damnfool dangerous, that's what it is," Metchnikovitch protested. "We'll have it out when I get back. Make sure Ivan is waiting for me."

"You do not give orders," Yerik said.

"If it weren't for me, you'd be floating face down in the Bay," snapped Metchnikovitch. "I've sheltered you, kept you out of the police's hands, financed this entire mad scheme. And without me, you'd never have come up with the idea of stealing the Fabergé baubles. Don't tell me what I can and can't do."

Slocum wished he could sow even more discord between the men, but he saw no easy way. They were quickly out of earshot. He studied the building again and decided this would be the best chance he was going to get anytime soon. Whatever he did had to be done quickly.

Crossing the street and going to the rear of the jewelry store, Slocum located the galvanized drainpipe. It provided a rickety ladder up to the second story, his feet often slipping away from the sides of the building. He stayed as close to the paint-slick wall as he could, both to take advantage of the gathering shadows and to keep from pulling the gutter from its moorings.

Strong fingers gripped a window ledge. Slocum reached out, stuck the toe of his boot into a wormhole, and balanced precariously to peer into the second-story window. In the room sat two Russians, one smoking a cigar that filled the room with dense blue smoke and the other cleaning an ancient revolver.

Slocum saw no sign of Juliana.

Swinging back and crawling up farther, Slocum came to the third floor. The window here was dark. Lifting the window and ignoring its wooden protests as it slid upward, he draped himself over the ledge and tumbled into the room. Hand on gun, he waited to see if anyone had noticed the noise and was coming to investigate.

The only sounds came from the floor below, where one of the men bellowed out a baleful Russian folk tune to the accompaniment of a balalaika. Even though he couldn't speak Russian, Slocum didn't have to be told the singing was off-key.

The room held a small bed and a clothes closet. On a table beside the bed stood a washbasin. Other than this sparse furniture the room was empty. Slocum went into the hall and checked out the other rooms on the floor. All were deserted. He tried to estimate how many men were staying here and decided on a minimum of ten.

The Colt in his hand didn't seem as powerful as before. Six bullets, ten men. He had been right when he decided stealth would free Juliana rather than brute force. Slocum found a spiraling stairway and went to the fourth floor. Light shone from beneath one door; all the other rooms were dark.

He pressed his ear against the door and listened. He knew this had to be Juliana's prison but didn't know if any of her captors were inside with her. The double locks and the heavy iron bar padlocked down showed that they held something very valuable within.

Silence. Then a soft rustle of cotton against cotton. A sigh. He couldn't tell if it came from a man or a woman.

Colt in hand, Slocum took the chance. "Juliana?" he called out. "You in there?"

"John!"

"Quiet. Listen close. There's no way I can get these locks off without bringing the whole herd of them down around my ears. Do you know where they keep the keys?"

"No. I didn't even know they had locks on the door. All I heard was the iron bar dropping."

"What about the window?"

"There are heavy shutters over the window. I don't think you can get them open. They might be nailed shut."

Slocum cursed under his breath. He had found Juliana after a day of going from one jewelry store to another on the hunch that a jeweler had been behind the theft of the Fabergé trinkets. From what he had overheard as Metchnikovitch argued with Yerik, that hunch held more truth than he'd thought.

Now he was stymied. Slocum saw no way of breaking Juliana out of her prison without attracting too much attention. Being on the top floor like this made escape even more difficult—and the time he had available before Metchnikovitch returned was running out.

"What we need is an army to get you out," he said. "But since there doesn't seem to be any handy, I'll take a crack at the door. Stand back." He thought he might be able to kick the door in if the hinges were weaker than the locks.

"John, wait, no," came Juliana's frantic words. "Not yet. They haven't made me tell where the box is, but..."

He didn't have to be told that the Russian countess

was weakening. Slocum had seen the kinds of tortures the Plains Indians were capable of meting out to their enemies. He doubted what Metchnikovitch and Ivan had done to Juliana was as bad, but he couldn't be sure. Then there was Yerik. Of this cold-eyed, merciless man he believed anything was possible. These Social Revolutionaries were dangerous fanatics who let nothing stand in the way of their mad schemes.

"Any ideas?" he asked.

"Prince Golitsyn might be back. If you can reach him he commands a squad of the tsar's top officers sent with us."

"A squad would be able to take the place apart," Slocum said.

"Dmitri is a master strategist. The finest in all of Russia," she said, pride tinting her words. Slocum decided he liked Dmitri Golitsyn even less, and he had still to meet the man.

"Where do I find the prince?" It galled Slocum to admit he was unable to rescue Juliana on his own, but facts were facts. He was outmanned and outgunned and needed reinforcements. This wasn't so much a retreat, he reckoned, as a regrouping.

Juliana rapidly told him where Golitsyn had rented a house and had bivouacked the squad of men.

"Don't worry, Juliana. I won't let them keep you longer than necessary."

"John," she said. "If there's any trouble, the egg is more important than my life."

Slocum snorted in disgust. No trinket, no matter how expensive or lovely, could compare with Juliana Rumyantsova.

"I'll be back soon," he said.

Slocum went to the rear of the house and pulled open the window. It opened more easily than the one on the third floor. He looked around and saw the coast was clear, then gripped the drainpipe and let himself down. Once he thought the rain gutter was ripping free, but it held. Enough. With luck, he'd not have to take this route to the top floor again. With Golitsyn and his troops, they'd have Juliana freed in nothing flat.

But somehow Slocum had misgivings that it would work out like that.

9

Slocum found the house on Mason Street without any trouble, but he didn't immediately go up to the white-washed front porch and knock on the door. It galled him no end that he had to go begging this Prince Golitsyn for aid. Not that Slocum was too proud to ask for help if he needed it—and it wasn't possible to free Juliana without *some* help—but this prince was an unknown character. All Slocum had to go on was what Juliana had said about him.

And truth to tell, Slocum didn't cotton any to someone whose fancy-ass silk dressing gown had been hanging in Juliana's wardrobe.

He watched the figures moving about inside the front room, dark silhouettes cast on the white lace curtains. From the way two of the men stood rigidly, Slocum guessed these were junior officers braced and at attention while their superior dressed them down for some minor disciplinary infraction.

Slocum knew he could wait no longer. If Juliana was to be freed before sunup, he'd have to hurry through this.

He rapped loudly at the front door. The quick steps of boots against wood floor came. The door opened. A young man stared at him without saying a word.

"Prince Golitsyn," said Slocum without preamble. "I want to speak to him. It's about Countess Rum-

yantsova." The young man winced. Slocum guessed
he had murdered the names with his American in-
flection, but that hardly mattered.

The man motioned Slocum inside. The interior of
the house was simple, almost too simple for anyone
to be living here. Slocum looked around and wondered
if Golitsyn and his men did anything more than use
this as a base. All the little touches showing habitation
were missing.

"Who are you?" asked a short man with heavily
waxed mustachios. He held himself ramrod straight
and carried a riding crop in one hand which he rapped
constantly against his right thigh. "Who are these people you asked after?"

"You must be Prince Dmitri Golitsyn," said Slocum. "There's not enough time to play your charades.
I know about the Fabergé boxes and eggs and all that
foolishness."

The prince made a vague gesture and two men with
drawn revolvers came from behind curtains to either
side of the entryway to the front room. Slocum wasn't
surprised to see them; he had already noted the toes
of their boots sticking out from under the draperies.

"You know nothing," said Golitsyn in clipped, sharp
tones. In Russian he gave a curt command. The two
armed men advanced.

"Juliana is being held by Metchnikovitch," Slocum
said in a rush. "I don't much care what you do to me,
but she needs your help." As the men took hold of
his arms and started him in the direction of the rear
of the house, he added, "The lady thinks highly of
your ability. Too highly, I'd say."

"Wait."

The men escorting Slocum halted.

Prince Golitsyn strutted up and eyed Slocum. A

small sneer curled one thin lip. All the while the riding crop rose and fell on his leg. Slocum wondered if he had developed a callus to protect his flesh.

"You say Metchnikovitch has her?"

Slocum only nodded. He pulled free of the two men and stepped up to Golitsyn. He towered over the man, topping him by almost a foot. This difference in height didn't seem to affect Golitsyn, but Slocum had never seen a small man who wasn't uncomfortable around a taller one. Some just hid it better than others.

"Come into this room. Sit. Tell me of her capture."

Slocum noticed that the guards trailed along, pistols still drawn. A quick look around the room told him which chair was the one reserved for the prince. Slocum turned and sat down on it, leaving Golitsyn unsure whether to order Slocum up and out or to accept it.

He accepted this petty defeat.

"We have not seen the countess in some time," said Golitsyn, perching himself on a writing table so that one knee-high boot could swing freely. The rapping with the riding crop increased to the point where Slocum wanted to rip it out of his hand and cram it down the man's throat. He forced himself to be calm. He had to convince Golitsyn of Juliana's plight or the woman would soon die at the Social Revolutionaries' hands.

"She managed to get back the miniature Fabergé jade pianoforte," said Slocum. "Metchnikovitch and two of his men—Ivan and Yerik—tried to kill her at Count Borov's funeral yesterday morning."

"If they tried to kill her, why do you now say they hold her captive? This does not make sense."

Slocum hadn't wanted to fully tell Golitsyn of his own involvement, but he saw he had to. "They had

me captive in a dockside warehouse and thought I
knew where the box was. I escaped. I reckon they
didn't find out I'd escaped until after the attempt on
Juliana's life. They found me gone, decided to kidnap
her and find out where the box was. Or maybe Ivan
decided she was the one who had it all along. He's
in a powerful sweat to get that box."

"Siberian jade is lovely," said Golitsyn, almost as
if he were lecturing a dimwit child.

"They have her on the fourth floor of Metchnikovitch's jewelry shop. I snuck in and talked with
her, but the locks were too strong for me to break
without bringing all ten of them down on my head.
Juliana suggested I get you and your squad of men.
Together we can take them."

"An interesting theory," Golitsyn said dryly. "I fear
that the Countess Rumyantsova must endure her im-
prisonment at these beasts' hands for some time further."

"But why? She'll be killed. Or she might give in
and tell them where the jade box is." Slocum couldn't
figure out what made Golitsyn tick. The man had little
feeling toward Juliana, even as a countrywoman.

"That she cannot do," said Golitsyn. He twirled
one mustache tip. "I have the Fabergé box. And with
luck, we will recover the rest of the items stolen from
St. Petersburg this very evening. Tsar Alexander has
entrusted this mission to me, and I will not fail."

"She'll die if you don't rescue her," said Slocum,
his anger rising. It was impossible for him to believe
Golitsyn wouldn't help Juliana, since it was obviously
within his power to do so.

"You do not understand our politics," said Golitsyn. "Tsar Alexander filled Semenovsky Square with
the spectacle of hanging the four who assassinated his

father. One of them was a woman. She was hanged as high as the rest. In Russia, all are treated equally. Countess Rumyantsova knew the dangers when she embarked on this sacred mission for our beloved tsar."

"If anyone's got the rest of your tsar's damned toys, it has to be Metchnikovitch. You can raid his place, eliminate all the Social Revolutionaries, *and* save Juliana."

"This is not where our sources tell us the remainder of the Fabergé treasures are. The sailor who stole the miniature pianoforte is dead. It is unfortunate for him, and also unfortunate for the thieves. This provided the best clue for us. We know where the Social Revolutionaries took them. It is not to this Metchnikovitch's shop. I have never heard his name before."

"I'm not lying."

"I cannot say what you are doing," said Golitsyn. "You are knowledgeable about things you have no business knowing. If I did not know the rebels so well, I would say you were sent as a diversion, a trick to make me follow the red herring, as you Americans say. But they are too suspicious, even of one another. They would never trust an American in any matter, even one so trivial as this." Golitsyn let out a staccato burst that Slocum took for laughter. "Also, they would know such a ploy would never work."

Slocum sat and fumed. Prince Golitsyn wasn't going to help him.

"All right, go off on your wild goose chase, but give me a rifle. A good one sighted in at a hundred yards. I can take out enough of them to at least give me a chance of rescuing Juliana myself."

This scheme appealed to Slocum. During the war there had been few, Yankee or Rebel, who were better shots, more effective snipers. Given a few minutes to set up a post, he figured on gunning down at least five of the Social Revolutionaries. With any luck, Yerik and Ivan would be among them. The confusion might let him get to the top floor and free Juliana.

It was desperate and even foolhardy for one man to try such a rescue, but if Prince Golitsyn wouldn't help, it was the best Slocum could come up with.

"Give you a rifle? That's rich," said Golitsyn, whapping the side of his boot with the riding crop. To one of the men with the leveled pistols, he rapped out something in Russian. Turning back to Slocum, he said, "You will be placed under arrest until we can sort out your story. Do not think to trick this young man. He is the son-in-law of General Tcherevin, the Chief of Imperial Police. He has been well trained."

Golitsyn rose and marched from the room without another word to Slocum. It took a few seconds for Slocum to realize matters had just got worse for Juliana. Not only wouldn't Golitsyn help rescue her, he had effectively prevented Slocum from trying anything in the woman's behalf, no matter how damnfool reckless.

Golitsyn and the others left. In a few minutes Slocum heard hoofbeats as their horses headed off into the night—in the wrong direction.

Slocum sat back in the chair and closed his eyes. His body ached, and the lack of sleep was starting to catch up with him. Worst of all was the pain he felt inside from failing so completely to help Juliana.

"Oh," he moaned, clutching his chest. Slocum ripped open his shirt and revealed the massive bruise that had spread during the day. "Shot. I been shot. Can't . . . Oh!"

He half rose, twisted about, and fell heavily to the

floor. The guard hesitantly moved closer, and Slocum acted, striking like a snake. His hand caught the Russian's bootheel just as the man started to put weight down on it. With a loud cry, the Russian army officer flung his hands into the air and crashed backwards to the floor. Slocum swarmed over him like ants on a picnic cake. A strong punch to the jaw made Slocum wince in pain as he bruised his knuckles, but it did the trick.

Rubbing his hand, Slocum stood up and looked at the unconscious guard. "The police chief should tell his men to be more careful. But what can you expect out of relatives?"

Slocum started to leave, then paused at the front door. He was no better off now than he was when he'd entered. Juliana wasn't going to be rescued if he didn't start using his head.

Remembering what Prince Golitsyn had said, Slocum turned and looked around. It took him almost an hour of intense searching before he found what he sought hidden away under a floorboard in an upstairs room. He balanced it on the palm of his hand, marveling at the detail and intricacy. He put the Fabergé pianoforte into his shirt pocket and left, heading back toward Metchnikovitch's shop.

If force was out of the question, there were other ways to skin a cat.

He found himself a roan horse still tethered out back, vaulted into the saddle, and rode like the wind, the slowly awakening city stretching around him as dawn again turned the horizon pink with promise. Slocum tried not to think of how long it had been since he'd had more than a quick nap.

Almost nodding off in spite of the horse's jarring gait on the cobblestones, Slocum arrived back at

Metchnikovitch's shop with enough energy to force himself into full alertness.

Slocum watched as the sleepy Russians stirred, then began moving about. One came outside and scratched himself, yawning gigantically. Slocum waited for his chance, then pounced. His Colt smashed down on the head of the man he had seen with Metchnikovitch the night before. Dragging the Social Revolutionary into the alleyway across from the jewelry shop, Slocum waited for the man to regain consciousness. it took only a few minutes. He congratulated himself on hitting only hard enough to stun.

Eyes darkened with madness glared at him. Slocum cocked the hammer and pointed the Peacemaker directly at the man's nose.

"Don't try anything dumb," he told him. "I don't even know if you understand English, but try this one on for size." He reached into his shirt pocket and pulled out the three-inch-long Siberian jade pianoforte. The Russian's eyes widened.

"That's right," Slocum said. "I have it. I'll trade. The Fabergé box for Juliana. Go tell Metchnikovitch."

He gestured with the gun. The man scampered across the street and loudly rapped on the front door. He vanished inside, and less than a minute later three men emerged, heading straight for the alleyway where Slocum stood.

The glint of sunlight off Yerik's thin-bladed knife did little to reassure Slocum that he was doing the right thing. Ivan and Metchnikovitch completed the trio.

"You are very busy man," Ivan said. "We had thought you long gone."

"Took you a while to find I'd slipped out of the warehouse," guessed Slocum.

"It did. No one has done that before. No American."

"There's always a first."

"Never mind this small talk. Show me the jade box," demanded Metchnikovitch.

Slocum pulled it out and placed it on the flat of his hand. He placed the muzzle of his Colt up against the pianoforte and cocked the six-shooter.

"Wait, don't!" started Metchnikovitch. "You'll—"

"I'll blow it to hell and gone is what I'll do unless you release the countess."

"She is prisoner of war," said Ivan.

"Then we're arranging a trade of prisoners," said Slocum. The snap of command came into his voice. "This box for Juliana."

The men said nothing for almost a minute. Each was lost in thought. Slocum tried to size them up. Yerik wanted nothing but to see blood flow, Ivan wanted the box more than anything else, and Metchnikovitch was truly pained at the idea of such a masterpiece being destroyed. But the jeweler did not seem inclined to free Juliana Rumyantsova for it.

Even among fanatics, there could be differences of opinion, Slocum noted. And these seemed to all work at cross-purposes.

"Decided yet?" asked Slocum.

"Get countess," ordered Ivan. "We make trade."

"No!" cried Metchnikovitch. "We have other plans for her. The box is valuable, but she is even more so. We can use her to our advantage."

"One," said Slocum.

"What?"

"Two. I blow this box to a million pieces on the count of three."

"Wait!" Ivan and Metchnikovitch cried at the same time. Metchnikovitch heaved a sigh and indicated that Ivan had won. The woman for the box.

Yerik trotted off to fetch Juliana.

"Don't take it so hard," Slocum said to Metchnikovitch. "You have the other items stolen. Even the Easter egg. All those ought to count more than even a Russian noblewoman."

"The workmanship is so lovely," said Metchnikovitch. "But there are higher callings in any revolution. The tsar must pay dearly for his cruel acts."

"Against the peasants?" asked Slocum.

"Against the Germans!" raged Metchnikovitch. "He hates Prussians, he hates Jews, he executes thousands in the name of Mother Russia."

"That why you're in this, too?" Slocum asked of Ivan.

The man shook his head. "Tsar is evil. He hanged my sister Sophia Perovskaya. He foolishly squanders money best used for feeding peasants. He drains Pinsk Marsh. He builds fantasy railroad across all of Siberia to connect St. Petersburg with Archangel."

"Let me guess," Slocum said tiredly. "This Sophia whatever you said was one of the bomb throwers who blew up Tsar Alexander's father."

"I am proud she assassinated tsar!" cried Ivan. For a brief moment Slocum saw the raging blaze of fanaticism in Ivan, too. It wasn't just Yerik who indulged in such mindless devotion to the Social Revolutionaries' cause of killing without quarter.

Slocum glanced over the men's shoulders and saw Yerik leading Juliana out. Yerik had her collar firmly in hand, his knife at her throat.

"John!" the woman cried, seeing him. "What are you doing?" The sight of the Fabergé box made her turn pale. "No, you can't. You can't give them that in exchange for my life. I will die for the Tsarina Marie Feodorovna!"

"You don't have to die for anyone, much less a spoiled queen," said Slocum. "Release her." He lifted the muzzle of the gun and stuck it inside the jade box. Yerik took his hand off Juliana's collar and stepped back, waiting. Slocum knew that knife for a deadly weapon. While it wasn't balanced for throwing, the razor-sharp edge could cause a world of damage if it were just tossed in his direction.

"Ivan, take the box from my hand." He figured Ivan was the least likely to do anything to jeopardize the box. Slocum was right.

The uneasiness mounted when the Russians had the Fabergé box and Juliana stood behind Slocum.

"Get up on my horse," Slocum told Juliana. He heard the horse complaining. He backed to the animal, gun still in hand, then vaulted up into the saddle behind her. "May I never see any of your ugly faces again," Slocum said. He jerked at the reins and spurred the horse down the alley. Two shots followed him, but he had gotten far enough away by the time Metchnikovitch and Ivan got their guns out.

His arms around Juliana, Slocum felt at peace with the world. Now all he wanted to do was find somewhere to hole up and sleep for a week. Or maybe a month. Everything was just great.

10

"We can't do it this way, John," Juliana Rumyantsova said in a voice that brooked no argument. She tried to turn in the saddle and look at him, but he held her too tightly. While it was nice feeling her slender body this close to his own, Slocum ruefully admitted to himself that he was holding on to her to keep from falling off the horse. His head spun and he was about ready to pass out. He'd been shot and bludgeoned and shanghaied and kidnapped and had raced about to rescue Juliana to the point that he and sleep were strangers.

"What do you mean?" he asked.

"The Fabergé box. I must get it back. We can't let Metchnikovitch have it."

"It was a good trade, you for a lousy hunk of stone."

"You'd say so," she said. Her hand rested lightly on top of his. She squeezed down gently. "But Tsar Alexander wants *all* the stolen treasures returned, not just his Easter egg."

"Seems like a lot of fuss over these trinkets," said Slocum. "More killing than they're worth. Hell, one dead over them's more than it's worth."

"Tsarina Marie Feodorovna puts great store in such things. And Tsar Alexander will do anything to please her."

"Nice she's married to such a thoughtful man," said Slocum, sarcasm entering his tone.

"The box is only part of the treasure stolen. If there's a way to recover all of it, we must."

"You want to go back and tackle all of Metchnikovitch's men? There are enough of those Social Revolutionaries in that jewelry shop to fight off a small army, even Golitsyn's, from what little I saw of it. And if many of the revolutionaries are like Yerik, they'll fight like cornered rats. I saw it too much in the war. Total devotion to a cause, right or wrong. No way of talking sense to any of them."

"Or to me," Juliana said. "I have been entrusted by the tsar to recover the stolen pieces. All of them. My life is forfeit if I return without them."

"So don't return. You speak English better than most folks, you're pretty, you're educated. Why return to such a tyrant?"

"Tsar Alexander is not a tyrant!" she said hotly. "That's what the Social Revolutionaries say, and they're wrong. They're the murdering swine who ought to be executed for crimes against Mother Russia."

Politics didn't much interest Slocum. And right now nothing interested him more than a few hours' sleep. Then he could be on the trail for Oregon.

"Take me back to my house," Juliana said.

"They tracked you there once. They might decide, now that they've got the jade box, to finish off what the bomb thrower started. I think Yerik likes to see people blown apart."

"They won't harm me. They'll be too intent on leaving San Francisco with the Fabergé collection."

"How'd they get it in the first place? I doubt your Tsar Alexander left it lying around on the kitchen table. From what little I've seen of Prince Golitsyn, it's not too likely anyone just walked off with it either."

"Dmitri is very efficient," she said primly.

"Why didn't he want to rescue you then?"

"Dmitri knows where his duty lies also. He thought the Fabergé egg was somewhere else and had to get it. Sparing even one man to save me might have endangered his mission. It must have been a difficult decision for him to make, but he made the proper one."

Slocum wanted to tell her how her hero Dmitri Golitsyn hadn't found the decision the least bit difficult and had thrown her to the wolves for nothing. While Slocum wasn't positive, he had a strong hunch that the Social Revolutionaries would carry out their original plans and take the Fabergé treasures to Fort Ross, where the former Russian colonists sympathized more with their goals.

Juliana was committed to retrieving the artworks. Slocum found himself more and more decided to get out of the entire mess and find a clean, long, straight road out of California.

"Got to find a place to sleep," Slocum said. He yawned and shook his head to force his eyelids open. It was a losing battle.

"My place. You can sleep there."

"Got shot there."

"By all the saints!" gasped Juliana. "You did! I had forgotten. How did you survive?"

Slocum found the cottage at the foot of Russian Hill and tethered his horse just inside the garden gate. "I'll show you," he told her. They entered. Slocum pointed to the bullet-blasted gold sunburst medallion she had given him.

"You were lucky," she said.

"You were luckier. If they'd killed me, you'd still be rotting in that room."

Juliana took a deep breath and left to go to the kitchen. Slocum heard her rustling around. He didn't care if she fixed coffee or a two-inch-thick steak with home fries. What he needed more than anything else in the world was sleep.

He slumped into the chair and was snoring in minutes.

In the distance he heard an argument. At first Slocum thought it was part of a nightmare he'd been living through. Ivan and Metchnikovitch stood to one side while Yerik menaced him with the flensing knife. Slocum had fled down the corridors of his dream and evaded them, only to find Golitsyn's leering face replacing theirs.

"Golitsyn," he muttered. Slocum turned and felt stiffened muscles protesting. He hadn't been able to get too comfortable in the chair, but it had been better than nothing at all to sleep on. Somehow even the effort of walking into the next room to lie down on the bed had been beyond his powers. Levering open one green eye, he peered forth and saw the diminutive prince slapping his riding crop firmly into the palm of his left hand.

Slocum stretched and got some of the soreness worked out. The sleep hadn't done much to restore his energy, but it had been better than none at all.

"So," said Golitsyn, planting himself firmly in front of Slocum. "He rejoins the land of the living."

"You're welcome," said Slocum.

"What?"

"I figured you were thanking me for rescuing the countess. Just said you were welcome."

Golitsyn drew back, the riding crop ready to lash out across Slocum's face. The prince stopped, seeing that Slocum's hand was resting on the butt of his pistol. He seemed to realize that long before the blow would land, a bullet would find its way to his heart.

"You fool!" raged Golitsyn. "You sacrificed the one item we have recovered. How dare you!"

"Looks to me like you haven't done all that powerful good a job," said Slocum. "The Fabergé pieces are stolen from under your nose, transported halfway around the world, and even then you can't do anything to recover them."

Golitsyn turned red in the face. His entire body shook with rage, and the riding crop started back for a blow.

"I like the way your mustache shakes when you get mad, too," said Slocum.

"Dmitri!" The sharp command from Juliana stayed the prince's hand once again. "He does not know what these items mean to Tsar Alexander. He is not Russian. He cannot know."

"He should not have meddled."

"Listen, half-pint," said Slocum, standing and peering down at the prince. "The Russian sailor stole something that had already been stolen. He died for it. His friend got killed because of it. There have been deaths coming out my ass, and all you can talk about is a jade box. Hell, have this Fabergé make another one."

"The box and the other items are replaceable," said Golitsyn. "The Easter egg is not. There is not enough time to fabricate another."

"Great," said Slocum. "So kill off a dozen people. That makes it all right."

"John, you don't understand." Juliana came over

and took his arm, more to make sure that he didn't draw down on Golitsyn than to calm him. She recognized how close to losing his temper he was. "We are a poor people. Symbols mean more to us than to those in this country. That our rulers have diamonds and emeralds and gold statues is a substitute for a second helping on the plate."

"Piss-poor one," Slocum said.

"But affordable by all of Russia. It gives the peasants something in which to take pride. Rob them of even this small measure of delight, of something to strive for, and you rob them of more than can be replaced—you rob them of faith, of hope, of belief in their tsar."

Slocum didn't buy that for an instant but wasn't going to argue the point with Juliana.

"Please, John," she said. "Russia is in upheaval politically. Tsar Alexander is trying to do great works."

"Draining marshland and building railroads halfway round the world?" He remembered what one of the Social Revolutionaries had said about crack-brained schemes. This Russian ruler seemed brimming over with them, and all Slocum could see was the way it kept money out of the peasant's pocket and food off his table.

Juliana's eyebrows shot up. "You have heard of the Pinsk Marsh works? It will give us farmland equal in size to the entire country of England. *That* will feed more peasants. But until then the gaudy presents give them hope of better days. The trans-Siberian railroad will open trade with the Orient and give a boost to our fishing fleets in the Pacific. But until the food begins to flow across the heartland of Russia, there must be a dream."

"Fabergé gives the dream," said Slocum. Listening to Juliana tell it made more sense than the Social Revolutionaries.

"There is that. And a creation of such beauty is an addition to our nation's heritage. It will not die with Alexander. It will live on. The hope it represents will live on."

"How'd the Social Revolutionaries get the Fabergé treasures in the first place?"

Golitsyn looked troubled by the question. Even Juliana hedged a little, then she squared her shoulders and answered.

"Social upheaval is on the rise in all of Russia," she said. "A riot outside the Anitchkov Palace along the Nevsky River drew away forces meant to guard the tsar."

"The Social Revolutionaries tried to assassinate him," said Golitsyn, pulling himself up to his full height. He didn't even come to Slocum's chin.

"The plot failed, but somewhere along the way the trinkets were taken," Slocum finished.

"Protecting our sovereign took all our attention," said Golitsyn. "We found two servants—Social Revolutionary sympathizers—who committed the actual theft."

Slocum envisioned their bodies dangling from nooses in the middle of a snow-packed Russian square. Maybe the peasants had cheered. Maybe not. That part he couldn't figure out.

"Seems to be an elaborate plot to get the booty out of Russia. That wasn't done on the spur of the moment."

"Those swine are everywhere, just like weevils infesting flour," muttered Golitsyn. "They were probably waiting for such a chance—that it was the theft of such art treasures could not be known by them in advance."

Slocum remembered what Metchnikovitch had said about financing the scheme, and maybe even planning it. Golitsyn made it sound as if the revolutionaries had just gotten lucky. Slocum snorted in disgust. He'd've thought more of the short man if he'd admitted he might have been snookered.

"The Social Revolutionaries," Juliana said. "The Fabergé boxes and frames and the Easter egg were smuggled from the palace. How they got to Archangel we have no idea. It must have taken a month or longer. Luck was with us when we found out about the ship sailing to San Francisco."

"Then that sailor, Stephan, stole the miniature pianoforte and all hell broke loose," Slocum broke in.

"It confirmed our belief that the items were aboard that ship. Stephan was not one of the traitors. He merely seized an opportunity. He must have realized that such a valuable box would be missed by those sending it to America and tried to recover it when he lost it to you in the poker game."

"How'd you find out about it?"

"I had been in touch with others on the ship and sought out Stephan. I happened by and saw you leaving the saloon and heard others speaking of what had occurred."

"So you figured on me having the box put away out of sight?" asked Slocum. He shook his head in wonder at all that had happened. Luck had played her hand throughout this.

"After I recovered the box, I gave it to Dmitri and tried to find what had happened to the other items. In that I failed. The Social Revolutionaries were alerted by Stephan's theft and removed all their ill-gotten Fabergé pieces before we could stop them."

"We wanted *them* as badly as the items," said Golitsyn.

Slocum didn't doubt that for a moment. He read as much into what wasn't being said as what was. The way it looked to him, Golitsyn had been the one responsible for the security and had failed. For whatever reason—love?—Juliana had agreed to help him recover the stolen property. The rest of it Slocum knew.

Actually, he knew more than Juliana and Dmitri. He knew where the Easter egg was likely to be taken.

Two officers rapped smartly on the door, then entered at Golitsyn's curt command. From their nervousness, Slocum guessed that something hadn't gone too well. They spoke rapidly in Russian. Slocum caught the despair in their eyes, in the way they held themselves.

Juliana turned to Slocum and told him all that had been said. "Metchnikovitch and the others have abandoned the jewelry shop. There was no chance to recover even the box, much less the egg."

"Pity," Slocum said, without much meaning it. If Golitsyn hadn't gone off on his wild goose chase Juliana could have been rescued and the Fabergé pianoforte would still be safe and sound.

"He is in league with them," Golitsyn said suddenly. His riding crop stabbed forth like an arrow, pointing directly at Slocum.

"Doesn't make much sense if I am," said Slocum. "Think on it. Why bother with Juliana's release? Just steal the box and give it over to them."

"You spy on us."

"Oh, Dmitri, he's right. John was merely acting

in what he thought were my best interests. He had no connection with them before he won the box from the sailor."

"No," said Dmitri Golitsyn. "They are clever. More cunning, perhaps, than we give them credit for. He is in our camp. He can spy on us and let them know our every move. You do not know he was ever the prisoner he claimed to be."

"He told me about the warehouse. He—"

Golitsyn cut her off with a brusque wave of the riding crop. "Precisely. *He* told you. This is a ridiculous story of the Social Revolutionaries kidnapping him from the ship after he had been shanghaied."

"They wanted the box and thought I knew where it was." Even as he said it Slocum saw it would do him no good. Prince Golitsyn had made up his pea brain, and nothing would change it now. He had found an American scapegoat to take the blame for his own failures and wasn't going to let anything like reason stand in his way.

"The exchange—you my darling Juliana for the jade box—was a ruse. They want to know of our progress in tracking them down and shooting them like the dogs they are!" Dmitri Golitsyn had worked himself into a fine pet. Slocum had taken enough. If he stayed another minute he'd likely punch the prince in the face.

"Juliana, I wish you all the luck in the world." He lightly kissed her on the forehead and stepped back. The woman's blue eyes widened in surprise. She hadn't expected Slocum to simply want to walk out of her life in this way.

"John, wait."

"Yes, John, wait," said Golitsyn, mimicking the countess. He pulled out a heavy Russian-made revolver that looked as if it weighed ten pounds. "Do not go. I think there must be an execution first. A traitor in our ranks. You, Slocum!"

Slocum went cold inside. Golitsyn would kill him and lay all the blame on the corpse. That part didn't bother Slocum; the part about being a corpse did.

Golitsyn stiffened his elbow, held the gun at arm's length, pointed the massive weapon at Slocum's head, and was drawing back on the trigger when Juliana grabbed the prince's wrist. The gunshot deafened Slocum, and the hot breeze of lead flying past his left ear told of how near death had been. Even to the last instant he hadn't believed the man would shoot him in cold blood.

Slocum reached for his own gun but found himself covered by three of the Russian army officers.

"Stop this!" cried Juliana. "He is not a spy!"

"He dies," said Golitsyn.

"Even if I know where the Fabergé egg is?" asked Slocum. Telling them looked to be the only way he'd ever get away with his hide in one piece.

Dmitri Golitsyn lowered his pistol with obvious reluctance, and Juliana stared at Slocum in surprise. At least he had their attention. But for how long?

11

"Where, John?" Juliana Rumyantsova asked. The combination of flaring hope and fear in her eyes told Slocum she was worried that Golitsyn might yet pull the trigger.

"Yes, Slocum, give me the answer."

"I'm not in cahoots with them," Slocum said quietly. "I overheard them talking when I was prisoner in the warehouse. I don't know for certain, but from everything I've heard and know, there's a good chance I know where they took the egg." The prince snorted derisively and made his mustache tips quiver. "Before I say another word, how do I know he won't plug me if I do tell you?"

"You have my word," said Juliana.

"I don't pretend to know about Russian royalty," Slocum said, his eyes fixed on Golitsyn, "but it seems to me that a countess isn't anywhere near as important as a prince. You can say what you want, but he can overrule you."

"Dmitri, give him your word. As an officer in the Imperial Russian Army and as a member of Tsar Alexander's Imperial Court." The prince's face reddened as he worked through the dilemma facing him. Slocum hoped it wouldn't take long. The man might rupture something and die if this went on. "Do it, Dmitri. For our tsar. For Tsarina Marie Feodorovna."

126

"If you tell us the truth, and if the Fabergé Easter egg is where you say, I will not harm you."

"That seems as good as I'm likely to get," said Slocum.

"It is more than you deserve," snapped Dmitri Golitsyn.

"Don't push your luck," said Slocum. "I'm the one with the information you need." Golitsyn started to lift his pistol again but stopped. He slammed it back into a highly polished leather holster hung cross-draw style on his left hip.

"It's some place you mentioned to me, Juliana," he said.

"But I don't know where they'd go," the dark-haired woman protested. "If I did, we would be there now."

"I heard Ivan saying they had a sizable following at 'the rancho.' This didn't set too well with me, a Russian using a Spanish word. He repeated it for Metchnikovitch." Slocum tried to duplicate what he'd heard. For a moment neither Juliana nor Golitsyn showed any sign that they understood. Then the prince burst out laughing.

"He means Rancho Chernykh!"

"That's what I said," Slocum muttered. He'd tried his best to repeat the name, but the Russian sounds had eluded him totally.

"I did tell you about Fort Ross, didn't I?" said Juliana, marveling at it. "The colony the Russian-American Company founded."

"I'd heard stories of it myself," said Slocum. "Up north of Bodega Bay."

"But wait," said Golitsyn, again turning suspicious. "The colony was abandoned in 1839. He would lead us on a time-wasting journey!"

"No, no, Dmitri. Many of the colonists returned to Russia then. The Farallons were abandoned with no one left, but Slavyansk kept some few of its people."

"The redwood fort above Port Rumyantsov," Slocum said, letting Juliana's family name roll off his tongue.

"Named for my great-uncle," the woman said to Golitsyn. "There are still colonists there, though they must consider themselves Americans now."

"California's been a state since 1850," pointed out Slocum. The two Russians ignored him.

"Ross Counter," Golitsyn said.

Seeing Slocum frown at this, Juliana translated. "Russian California. The idea has never quite died in some circles."

"These remaining colonists would want to see California part of Russia?" he asked.

"Perhaps so. Their sympathies would lie with the peasants," said the prince. "Many who returned felt that the tsar did not support them fully enough, that he allowed the colony to fail. This is untrue, of course. The colony never produced enough grain to make itself an asset to the motherland."

"Fort Ross is about thirty verst from Bodega Bay," said Juliana to Golitsyn. "We can ride for it and be there within four days."

"Three. We ride with the wind like Cossacks!"

"Verst?" asked Slocum.

"Thirty verst is, oh, about twenty miles," said Juliana.

He shrugged. This was no concern of his now. He had passed along what little information he had. What the Russians intended doing with it was their business.

"I'll be going now."

Golitsyn's gun slipped once more from its holster.

"Wait." The coldness of the command froze Slocum. He wished now he'd taken the chance and shot Dmitri Golitsyn down like a dog. Any man who broke his word like this was not a man at all.

"Dmitri, you promised," said Juliana, shocked.

"We cannot allow him to leave. I still believe he is in with the Social Revolutionaries."

"He isn't," maintained Juliana.

"And if he isn't," Golitsyn went on smoothly, "we still cannot risk allowing him to walk away freely. He might go to the American authorities with this tale."

"Can't you use a little police help?" Slocum asked. That was the last thing on his mind, but he wondered at Golitsyn's insistence that the police be kept out of this. While he had seen the corruption of the San Francisco police, and their "specials" taking bribe money, a federal marshal might be just what the doctor ordered for riding into Fort Ross and recovering the Fabergé egg.

"I understand," Juliana said wearily. To Slocum she explained. "Tsar Alexander has decreed that Russia is for Russians. This means that we must do everything for ourselves without outside help."

"Seems like this is getting you in hot water," observed Slocum. "While I don't think highly of them myself, the police in San Francisco could have caught Metchnikovitch and the others in nothing flat. They might even have enjoyed cracking a few Russian heads open."

"It is more than a political dictum," said Juliana. "Pobedonostsev, the Procurator of the Holy Synod, has also decreed it."

"The Black Tsar," muttered Golitsyn.

"Are you saying this is a religious matter, too?"

Slocum didn't like the way the Russians got their politics and religion all mixed together. "That's foolish."

"The Black Tsar is Alexander's tutor and has held his ear in political matters over long years. When Pobedonostsev speaks, Tsar Alexander listens."

"Something else that Dmitri has not mentioned," said Juliana, "is that we are both members of the Holy League. Prince Belosselsky organized it to protect the tsar in all matters. Our instructions in this come from him to eliminate the Social Revolutionaries—"

"—and from Tsar Alexander to recover the Fabergé egg," finished Golitsyn.

Slocum's head spun. He knew he had caught only the barest fringes of the politics and religion that must go on in the Russian Imperial Court, and even this confused him. Life was so much simpler in America. No kings or tsars or princes or intrigue. Slocum had no good idea what went on in Washington, but it wasn't anything this devious.

He longed to be away from all of them—even Juliana Rumyantsova—and back into the wilderness where he understood how to survive. Tracking a deer and killing it involved skill, not back-stabbing politics. Trapping for furs was hard work, but religion didn't muddy the waters. A moose didn't care squat about fancy Easter eggs or peasants or anything but finding another meal and making more moose. These were things Slocum cared about too. He felt more at home with the antlered elk than any of these fine, honorable Russian nobles.

"We leave immediately for Fort Ross," said Golitsyn. "We must not allow them time to hide the treasure. If they do so we may never recover it."

"Can't we wait a while longer?" asked Slocum.

Tiredness still dulled his senses, and he longed to stretch out on Juliana's bed, either with her or without her, and rest until moving about wasn't such an effort.

"Now."

That settled it. Slocum rode the roan with Juliana beside him. Prince Golitsyn and two of his officers brought up the rear, while a half-dozen more ranged ahead. Of the son-in-law of General Tcherevin whom he had escaped from the night before, Slocum saw no sign.

At least there was something to be thankful for. Wondering if Golitsyn would shoot him in the back was bad enough. The angry young officer would have fired without hesitation.

Slocum dozed in the saddle.

"He is dangerous," said Dmitri Golitsyn to Juliana.

"Yes," the woman whispered. "Very dangerous."

"That is not what I meant," the prince snapped. "He is in league with the Social Revolutionaries. He plots our downfall even now."

"He sleeps now," she said. "I do not think he is capable of the intrigues you hint at."

"I hint at nothing," said Golitsyn. "He had the box and gave it back to Metchnikovitch."

"Metchnikovitch is a fool," the dark-haired woman said. "They all are. Their movement borders on complete anarchy. Some value only killing, others have bizarre political ideals, and still others are misfits that have no other place in society. That is the Social Revolutionaries' weakness. They cannot have a true leader."

"They can still do damage. Tsar Alexander II is dead from their bombs."

"But those responsible are dead, too. I saw their

chemist—what was his name?—ah, yes, Zhelyabov, with his neck stretched in the square. And the others. All dead."

"There is danger," insisted Golitsyn.

Juliana looked at the small man and smiled. "It is your duty to protect our *bychok*. You are good at it, Dmitri. But do not think to carry your duty too far afield."

"That is no way to speak of our tsar. 'Little bull,' indeed." He tapped his riding crop against his horse's neck and trotted on ahead. The change in tempo awoke Slocum, who looked around, still groggy.

"You return to the land of the living," Juliana greeted him.

Slocum wasn't too sure about that. This wasn't what he called good rest. He'd have preferred to find a nice haystack, to stretch out and gaze up at the clear blue sky and then drift away for a dozen hours of hard sleep.

"Dmitri thinks you are leading us into a trap."

"Dmitri's brain is in proportion to the rest of him— half-sized."

"He is no half-wit," Juliana chided, but Slocum noted she wasn't angry that he'd insulted the prince. "Few in Russia are more capable field commanders than Prince Golitsyn."

"Doesn't know spit about riding through terrain like this, though," said Slocum.

"Oh," she said. "How would you do it differently?"

Slocum pointed. "Those rock formations could hold an entire army. Assuming this is a well-traveled path to Fort Ross, why hasn't he considered that Ivan and the others might have lookouts posted?"

"Speed is our ally."

"They've got a head start on us," pointed out Slocum. "They might decide to lay a trap for the unwary. Half-pint's about as unwary as any I've seen. You'd think he had an entire army at his beck and call instead of a few flashy cavalry officers."

"You sound as if you know something about tactics."

Slocum started to tell Juliana about his captaincy in the Confederate army, then pushed it aside. Those were pages in a history book long closed.

"Common sense," he answered.

"We will find Fort Ross without difficulty," Juliana said, but the worried expression on her face showed Slocum he had planted doubts in her mind. "This country is so different from what I am familiar with," she said, changing the subject. "I wish I could explore more fully."

"What are you used to?"

Juliana laughed, and Slocum felt the magic in that simple, cheerful sound. With the pines and the soft, damp wind and the feel of freedom around them, he couldn't have asked for much more in life—unless it was getting rid of Golitsyn and his soldiers to be alone with Juliana.

"Not riding," the woman said, raising up in her stirrups and rubbing her pert behind. "Society life is more in keeping with a night in St. Petersburg. Dining at Cubat's Restaurant. Gay times with Vladimir and Alexis."

"Who are they?"

"Tsar Alexander's brothers. Both are grand dukes. Vladimir is the president of the Academy of Fine Arts and the Commander of the Imperial Guard. He knows nothing about either. And Alexis? He is the Grand Admiral of the Russian fleet."

"And he can't even swim?" asked Slocum.

"You would fit right in, with your quick wit," Juliana said, smiling. "Alexis may have seen a ship once. He is more occupied with his ménage à trois with the Duchess of Leuchtenburg and her husband."

Slocum didn't know exactly what Juliana meant, but he made a good guess. "Do you hang around with that crowd?"

"When I am in St. Petersburg. That is where the real life is. Café society. Tsar Alexander is, as I have said, very much the peasant in his tastes."

Slocum rode with eyes straight ahead, cut off from the woman. She lived in a world entirely different from his. He could no more fit into the café society she loved than she could enjoy the hunt, the pleasure of a roasted haunch of venison, and the brains for dessert. Slocum didn't even know if she enjoyed being away from odor-ridden San Francisco and into clean air once more.

Before Juliana could say a word, Slocum held up his hand and silenced her. He pointed. The flash of sunlight on steel came again.

"What is it?" she asked.

"Maybe nothing. Or maybe it's Ivan and his party. If so, we might be in for trouble unless..."

"Unless?"

"That might be a guard they left behind to watch their trail. If it is, he's clumsy. I might be able to stop him before he can tell anyone he's seen us."

"Has he?"

"Not if he's anywhere near as good as your prince."

"I will tell Dmitri you are going to stop this guard."

"Thanks, Juliana. I don't cotton to the notion of Golitsyn using that cannon of his to backshoot me." Even as the countess rode ahead to speak with Golitsyn, Slocum's sharp eyes were picking out a path up the flinty slopes that led to a ridge where he might be able to overtake the man riding guard for the Social Revolutionaries.

Slocum cut away and rode off. The Russian soldiers in the party never even noticed. Only when Golitsyn told them did they see that Slocum had melted into the pines and was gone.

He would have chuckled over this except his entire concentration focused now on finding the spoor left by the lone rider and tracking the man down. Slocum rode for almost a mile along the ridge before he saw the tiny trail winding down the other side—a single hoofprint in a patch of half-melted snow and mud alerted him. If that had been made earlier, the snow melting in the bright California sun would have erased it.

Slocum picked up the pace. He was sure now that the guard had spotted their party and was riding ahead to Fort Ross to warn Ivan and Metchnikovitch and the others. If he succeeded it meant bloodshed that Slocum wasn't prepared to accept.

An hour of riding brought Slocum much, much closer to his quarry. Increasing signs of recent passage began to appear, and Slocum knew he had the man when a shot rang out. Tiny shards of stone exploded next to Slocum's ear. He was off his horse and onto the ground, as if he'd been struck. Again the guard had been careless and allowed the glint of sunlight off metal; Slocum had been prepared for the shot.

He lay still, pistol in hand, waiting, listening. The hesitant sound of a man approaching told the story. His would-be assassin wanted to see who he had shot.

Slocum judged distances and rolled over, revolver cocked and finger tight on the trigger.

"Good to see you again, Ivan."

The Russian stopped and stared. "But I shot you!"

"You're not that good a shot. I knew it by the way you left such a broad trail. Put down that rifle." Ivan visibly shook as conflict tore at his guts. To drop the rifle meant capture. To try and stop Slocum meant death.

He dropped the rifle.

"What do you do with me now?" asked Ivan, totally demoralized. "Send me back to Russia to be hanged? I am proud to die for the cause!"

"Can all that," said Slocum in disgust. "Your politics gives me a headache. For the moment, we're just going back to visit with Prince Golitsyn."

"That pig."

"Can't say I hold him in much higher esteem, but he's the one leading this whole sheebang. He deserves to have a word or two with you."

"I will tell him nothing."

"Admirable sentiments, but not too practical. There are Indians in these hills able to make any white man talk within a couple days of trying. Can't say I like their methods much, but they work."

"You would torture me?"

"I'm saying Golitsyn might."

"What do you want from me?"

"Just about what Golitsyn would ask. If you're heading to Fort Ross. What fortifications they have there. Strength. Number of guns." Slocum paused, then added, "And where the Fabergé egg is."

Ivan snapped to attention and stood with eyes unblinking and not a muscle twitching. Slocum heaved a sigh. He had been afraid it'd be like this. Fanatics.

He motioned with his pistol and started Ivan walking back. Slocum found his horse grazing at a dry patch of grass a hundred yards down the slope and mounted up. When he marched Ivan back to Golitsyn, a silence so heavy he could cut it with a knife fell.

Juliana was the first to speak. "See, Dmitri? He did not run off to join them."

"This is a trick. They sacrifice one of their own to make us believe Slocum is our ally."

"Dmitri," said Slocum, "you have the most suspicious mind of any cayoose I ever saw. I don't rightly care if you believe this or not. But it's the truth. Ivan's the only guard they had on the trail. I stopped him from telling a soul that we're on the way. And I think he might know something about where the egg's being kept and how it's guarded." Slocum prodded Ivan with the toe of his boot. "Don't you, Ivan?"

The man said nothing.

Golitsyn motioned. Two of the Russian soldiers dismounted, took the captive to a tree, and tied him securely.

"We camp here for the night," said Golitsyn. "We interrogate the prisoner."

"You're welcome," spoke up Slocum.

"What?"

"I said, Prince, that you're more'n welcome for me going out and stopping him for you." Golitsyn turned away, the tips of his mustaches trembling.

Looking at the small man's retreating back, Juliana said, "It is not wise to insult him like that. He can be very vindictive."

"Insulting him is about the only fun I've been having. This isn't much of a picnic."

"Fun?" Juliana asked, a slow smile brightening her face. "Perhaps we can discover ways of having fun. Together."

"Be looking forward to it," said Slocum. He jerked around when a high, piercing scream disturbed the

serenity of the woods. He dismounted and ran to where
Golitsyn had tied Ivan to a tree. The captive's head
drooped forward, and the man's heavy body had
slumped against the ropes binding him.

"What'd you do to him?" demanded Slocum.

"An old Cossack trick for making unwilling prisoners speak the truth," said Golitsyn. "It is no concern
of yours."

Slocum had to agree. His mind drifted from the
dead Ivan to the miles of wintery California leading
to Oregon. He had no allegiance to men who killed
prisoners. Slocum had decided that matter for himself
when he rode with Quantrill. Bill Quantrill had started
a new type of warfare—no prisoners, whether they
be men, women, or children. He slaughtered them
all. The senseless murder of innocents was something
Slocum had never gotten used to, even as he did some
of it himself. Those were hard men, and he lived in
hard times.

There had been no need for Golitsyn to kill Ivan,
except that he shared the single most sickening trait
of Bloody Bill Anderson and Quantrill and Cole
Younger and all the others. He enjoyed death.

The trail north looked more inviting all the time.

"Slocum," the prince said in a soft, menacing voice,
"I can read you like an opened book. You think to
slip away as you did to capture this animal. You will
not be allowed to do it. One of my officers will watch
you until we arrive at Fort Ross."

"I'm no further use to you. Fort Ross's not more
than two days' easy ride from here." Slocum heard
the crashing of waves against the nearby shoreline.
Bodega Bay wasn't too far, and Fort Ross lay only
twenty miles north of that. If he turned inland and
skirted the Sierras, went through the redwood forests

and past Lava Plateau, he'd be in Oregon in less than a week.

"I still believe you are in league with them. You might have convinced the impressionable Countess Rumyantsova of your sincerity, but I think you are lying. And it is *I* whom you must deal with."

Slocum widened his stance and shifted his hips slightly to bring his Colt around a little on his hip. The feel of a rifle muzzle against the back of his head made him reconsider.

Prince Golitsyn snapped a command in Russian. The officer behind Slocum took the Colt from the holster.

"Escape is futile. We ride to Fort Ross." Dmitri Golitsyn looked at Slocum and smiled without any humor. "And there, Slocum, there I think you will die."

12

Slocum was aware of the gun pointed at his spine the rest of the way to Fort Ross. He found himself considering escapes and other ways of turning the tables on Golitsyn, but he didn't try any of them. In a way he didn't quite understand, Slocum wanted to see this madness through to the end. Not for Juliana Rumyantsova, though she was an important part, but more out of curiosity.

The Siberian jade miniature pianoforte had been lovely—and men had died for it. What was the Fabergé Easter egg like that brought revolutionaries and Russian loyalists halfway around the world? Slocum tried to picture what this creation must be and failed.

"If I were in Fort Ross, I'd have guards posted on either of those rises," Slocum said, pointing out the spots. He had been carefully watching and hadn't seen any sign of life, but that didn't mean all the settlers were as careless as Ivan had been. If anything, they were probably good frontiersmen and trackers. They'd lived here for almost fifty years and must have learned every rock and tree, every Indian and game trail in the territory.

"They have no reason to suspect we are coming," said Golitsyn. "But we watch. Oh yes, Slocum, we watch." The man's eyes bored into Slocum, accusing, probing.

"Juliana," said Slocum, ignoring the prince, "he still thinks I've warned them somehow. You want to try and convince him I have no interest in this?"

"John, he is only carrying out orders given him personally by Prince Belosselsky—and the tsar. Dmitri will accomplish his mission. I am sure of it now. And it will be with your help."

"Maybe with my help, but it's not voluntary help, not with a gun pointed at my head."

"I've talked to him. He won't be swayed." She reached over and touched his arm. The contact was brief but exciting. Slocum decided curiosity about the egg and Juliana were keeping him with Golitsyn and the Russians.

The lead officer motioned down into the valley. Slocum and Juliana reined in beside him. Golitsyn was already squinting into the setting sun, trying to get the lay of the land. The trail they followed wound back and forth down a steep slope to a meadow where Fort Ross stood looking out over the Pacific Ocean. The redwood walls needed repair in places, showing that they weren't often attacked. The Indians in northern California were peaceable enough, and the Nez Percé never strayed this far south. The meadow ran to a cliff overlooking a cove where a ship might safely harbor. Scant evidence of recent dockings showed. Fort Ross was isolated, and, from the looks of the men working in the fields to the north of the fort, readying the ground for winter wheat, this suited them just fine. They were prosperous and healthy and probably happy.

Slocum wondered if all that would change with Golitsyn's coming.

"We will be seen if we stand here much longer," Golitsyn said. He motioned, and the small band rode

down the trail and found a level area barely wide
enough for them to camp. From a vantage point higher
on the slope, they could mount a watch on the fort.

"It will be safe enough for the night," said Golitsyn.
"As long as Slocum does not slip away to warn Metchnikovitch and the others."

"Golitsyn," Slocum said tiredly, "I've told you over
and over that I have no interest at all in Russian politics. I couldn't care less if you or Metchnikovitch or
the King of Siam rules Russia. And I sure as hell don't
care about your tsar and his Easter gifts."

"Dmitri," said Juliana, stopping the man from
drawing his gun. "He is being honest."

"He is being impudent!"

"Same difference, it looks," said Slocum. "I don't
know why you want me along like this, but you have
something sticking in your craw. Spit it out and let's
talk it through."

"Those are Russian settlers below," said Golitsyn.

"I'd call them Americans, since they live in the
state of California, but I'll admit they are of Russian
descent."

Golitsyn ignored him. "I am empowered by their
tsar to kill all of them, if necessary, to regain the
Fabergé egg. But they are fellow countrymen. To
slaughter them because of the Social Revolutionaries
is doubly galling."

Slocum snorted derisively.

"John, please. Dmitri is matching your honesty in
this. Hear him out."

Slocum tried to figure out Juliana's part and failed.
She was a lady-in-waiting to Tsarina Marie Feodo-
rovna, but how far did such duty go? To killing others?
Obviously. To dying herself? It looked that way. Slo-

cum understood patriotism, giving one's life for country and firm belief. While he hadn't believed in slavery, the issues in the war were more complex than that one, and Slocum fought for those while believing the slavery question would die on its own sooner or later. What he didn't follow was dying over a trinket. Even if this Fabergé Easter egg was the most expensive and elaborate jewel in the tsar's crown, dying for it was silly.

"I," Golitsyn said, "will not sleep easily at night knowing I have killed countrymen duped into harboring those barbarians who have stolen the tsar's treasures."

"Get to the point," said Slocum.

"This is the point. We watch, we see much. If I mount an attack, we will destroy Fort Ross and kill most of the people. We will regain the egg, but the burdens will be great."

"You just want the egg back without having to bloody your hands."

"There is nothing wrong in that. Unlike the Social Revolutionaries, we live by rules and possess a moral standard. As an officer of the Imperial Army, I am entrusted with protecting the lives—and property— of all Russians loyal to the tsar."

Slocum thought of Ivan hanging by the ropes back on the tree trunk. Golitsyn might speak of morals and highfalutin philosophies, but he was a killer and enjoyed death.

"You should have found youself a federal marshal to go after Metchnikovitch," said Slocum.

"No!" Golitsyn twirled his mustache tips and began pacing back and forth. Slocum thought of a shooting gallery back in San Francisco where the city slickers could take potshots at moving clay figurines. "Tsar Alexander has declared this to be a Russian matter. I have told you that."

"Hard to accept."

"You are adept at moving unseen," said Golitsyn. "While I do not fully trust you, I must ask that you accompany me into Fort Ross to find the egg."

Slocum laughed. "This is a Russian matter, or so says your tsar, and yet you're willing to let me help you? With a gun at my head? You've got to be joking."

"Dmitri, let me speak with him." Juliana took Slocum's arm and guided him to a spot overlooking the fort. The sun was setting over the Pacific, casting golden rays across the heaving, wave-dotted surface. Already cooking fires were blazing around the fort from half a hundred houses nestled in the woods around the wheat fields. This was a nice place to settle down, Slocum thought, if that was what you sought.

"It is only with great difficulty that Dmitri can even speak with you," Juliana said. "I have convinced him that merely recovering the Fabergé egg is not enough. We must do it with the least disturbance of those peoples' lives." She pointed to the settlement. "They might not favor Tsar Alexander or even be Russian citizens any longer, but they are still our people."

Slocum perched on a rock and watched as several men on horseback left Fort Ross and rode north. They didn't even bother barring the fort's gate behind them. It stood open, inviting. Whatever else the Social Revolutionaries had brought to this community, they hadn't brought fear or doubt. Life continued in its even pace.

"I reckon I understand that," he said.

"I knew you would. Dmitri wants to sneak into the fort and find the egg, steal it, and get out without harming anyone. While the soldiers with him are fine military officers—the best!—they are more familiar with fighting in the Crimea than such...such..." Juliana struggled for the word.

"Sneaky fighting," supplied Slocum.

"Indian-style scouting," she said. "We do not know the extent of the Social Revolutionaries' contact with the settlement. All there may be in sympathy with the rebels, or none may be. We cannot say what lies they have told."

"I won't be all that good in finding out. I don't speak Russian."

"True, but Dmitri does. The two of you together will be able to find out all we need to...to prepare."

Slocum had to admit the idea made sense. Never attack blindly if you could get good reconnaissance. He had the skill to sneak into Fort Ross and look around without being caught—Golitsyn didn't. But if they happened to overhear a conversation in Russian, Slocum wouldn't be able to tell if it meant disaster or that all they needed to know was carelessly being gossiped about—Golitsyn could. Still, Slocum didn't cotton to the idea of having Golitsyn with him. The man's trust of Slocum was about as small as his body.

"There are conditions," Slocum said. "I get my gun back."

"Dmitri will see that is a fair condition."

"If we can get the egg without harming anyone, we do, and that ends it. No retribution afterward on the Social Revolutionaries. I don't much like any of them, but I won't see them murdered like Golitsyn did Ivan."

"That," admitted Juliana, "might be more difficult. If Dmitri has the Fabergé egg, the temptation to carry the war to the Social Revolutionaries will be great."

"Talk to him about it. And there's one last point."

"Yes?" Juliana's blue eyes gleamed and her face softened. Her lips begged to be kissed. Slocum resisted the temptation, but it took all his will power.

"Whether or not we get the egg, I'm free to ride on. This isn't my fight."

Juliana lowered her gaze and nodded. "I understand, John. You have been more helpful than anyone could have expected."

"I did it for you," he said, putting his finger under her chin and lifting her face to again look into those beautiful eyes. The hard days on the trail hadn't dimmed Juliana's loveliness. If anything, it had only enhanced her natural good looks. "I don't understand your world of assassination bombings and risking your life for a rich ruler's toy, but I do understand you're one hell of a fine woman."

"John, I—"

"Slocum! Juliana!" called Golitsyn. "There you are. Have you made a decision on the matter Countess Rumyantsova presented?"

"I'll do it. You want to tell him my conditions?" asked Slocum.

Juliana spoke rapidly in Russian. Golitsyn at times became so agitated he stamped about and swung his riding crop at rocks and low shrubs. His mustache tips began to droop, though, and Slocum recognized defeat for the small prince.

"Very well, Slocum. I will give you back your pistol. This does not mean I trust you."

"Getting my gun back doesn't mean I trust you, either, Prince. I figure to go down the slope in another hour or so. There're no sentries posted, and by then most folks will have chowed down and settled into their routine just before going to bed."

"Is this not a dangerous time to go to the fort?"

Golitsyn asked. "With people still awake, we might be more easily discovered. You do not think to trick me like this, do you?"

"Know what else I see down there, Prince? Dogs. Lots of them running around loose. If a dog starts barking, its owner's not going to pay no nevermind if he thinks it's just one of his neighbors passing by. If that same dog starts barking come midnight or even later, that man's going to get his rifle down and go to see what's causing the commotion. We stand a better chance of finding what we want, and without being caught, if we do it my way."

"Dmitri, you yourself said he was more expert in such matters." Juliana added a few words in Russian. The clouds darkening Golitsyn's face did not lighten.

"I am unconvinced, but we will do it your way. I warn you, Slocum, the first sign of betrayal and I kill you."

"I'll keep it in mind," Slocum said dryly. "Speaking of food, I'm a mite hungry myself. Why not have something before we go off to do a night's work?"

Slocum noted that Golitsyn stewed even more in his juices when Juliana resisted the prince's attempt to put an arm around her waist. She glanced at Slocum, then hurried on into their small camp. Just what it was—or wasn't—between the two Slocum couldn't decide. He still remembered the silk dressing gown Juliana had given him at her house near Russian Hill. Maybe he had just jumped to the wrong conclusion that it belonged to Dmitri Golitsyn. However the trail ran, Slocum found himself caught up in Golitsyn's distrust and Juliana's uneasiness with both him and the Russian prince around together.

They ate in silence, stars popping out in the dark, wintery California sky. A heavy wind began blowing

off the Pacific, and the temperature dropped rapidly.
Slocum pulled his coat tighter around himself to keep
out the sea breezes. He thought that, while he was
still colder than a well digger's destination, he'd be
a hell of a lot colder if he'd ended up shanghaied and
on the ship heading for China.

Thinking on that, he had to smile.

"What's so funny, John?" Juliana asked.

"Just thinking about Shanghai Kelly," Slocum said.
"I hope he enjoys the scenery."

"What do you mean?"

"Nothing," he told the woman. To Golitsyn he
said, "Time to be moving. They'll have finished off
all their chores and eaten down there. We can be in
and out before they know what's what."

The prince nodded curtly. As he started for his
horse, Slocum said, "On foot. We go on foot. Quieter."

Golitsyn was a cavalry officer, and Slocum took
perverse glee in making the prince walk, not that he
fancied it so much himself. But it was a better way
of scouting.

"My gun," Slocum said, not moving when Golitsyn
went to the edge of their camp.

Golitsyn motioned. One of the Russian officers
returned Slocum's Peacemaker. Slocum checked it,
made sure rounds rode in all six chambers—if he got
into a fight he wanted the extra round under the hammer—and slipped it into his holster. Without a word
he started off past Golitsyn, picking his way and moving as silently as a shadow across a shadow.

They didn't speak as they worked their way across
a winter wheat field newly plowed and readied for
fertilizer and seeding. A curious dog or two came up
barking, sniffed them out, and then strolled off in the
mistaken belief that they belonged. Slocum looked at

Golitsyn and flashed the Russian an "I told you so" smile.

The gates to Fort Ross stood open. They slipped inside without being detected. Huddling together, Slocum asked, "The layout's not what I'd call usual. Where's the main quarters most likely to be? There?" He pointed out a squat building set off to one side.

"Yes," Golitsyn answered. "The commandant's safe is a likely place for the Fabergé items."

"A safe? Do you think we'll have to blow it open?" Golitsyn shrugged and shook his head. This was Slocum's show, not his. Slocum stooped over and duck-walked toward the one-story building. Peering inside, Slocum's heart almost jumped out of his chest. Staring directly at him was Metchnikovitch.

Slocum knew better than to make a sudden move. He sank down slower than molasses, waiting for a hue and cry to go up. When it didn't come, he relaxed. The lamps inside had blotted out his image and hidden him enough from Metchnikovitch and the eight other Social Revolutionaries gathered around the table.

"Didn't see any safe," he whispered to Golitsyn. "But Metchnikovitch and the others are inside." They hugged the deepest shadows when three men walked past them not a dozen paces away.

"More Social Revolutionaries," said Golitsyn. "That makes almost a dozen of them. We must attack Fort Ross—at dawn!"

"Wait," said Slocum. "We still don't know where the booty is. Looting and killing might not get the egg. Would Metchnikovitch destroy it just to keep it from being recovered?"

"Yes."

The word told Slocum all he needed to know. This wasn't a rational fight. Metchnikovitch, even though

he was a jeweler and respected fine work, was enough
of a fanatic to destroy the Fabergé pieces rather than
let Tsar Alexander recover them. Why any of these
men—or women, Slocum thought, adding Juliana—
would die for a toy egg was beyond him, but those
were the facts.

"If we find the safe, we might be able to work out
another plan," he told Golitsyn.

"You can crack this safe and get out the stolen
treasures?"

"Can't say till I see what I'm up against." Slocum
motioned him to silence when three of the Social
Revolutionaries left.

"Metchnikovitch!" whispered Golitsyn.

"He'd know all about the safe, wouldn't he?" Slocum said, thinking out loud. He restrained Golitsyn
from shooting the man down. Whatever animosity
existed between loyalist and revolutionary, Golitsyn
was still enough in control of his emotions not to
jeopardize their mission.

Slocum tugged on Golitsyn's sleeve. They drifted
along behind the three as the Social Revolutionaries
left the fort and started along a trail leading to one of
the houses. Before they got halfway to the house,
Slocum indicated to Golitsyn that they should attack.
Whatever else he thought about the banty rooster of
a man, Slocum couldn't fault his courage.

Slocum hurried up behind one of the men and
slugged him with his pistol before he turned. Golitsyn
wrestled another to the ground and knocked him out
with a short, powerful right to the chin. The crack
that echoed through the redwoods sounded loud enough
to wake the dead, but only those on the path heard
it.

Slocum cocked his gun and leveled it at Metchnikovitch, the only one from the fort still on his feet. Their attack had come swiftly and silently, and the element of surprise had allowed Slocum and Golitsyn to seize prisoners.

"Don't even think on it," Slocum cautioned Metchnikovitch. The Russian jeweler's hand drifted toward a pistol hung in a shoulder holster. Slocum disarmed him and tossed the small-caliber weapon into the forest.

"No sound," said Golitsyn. "I will kill you if you attempt to cry out."

"He knows that, Prince," said Slocum. "Metchnikovitch wants to play along with us, don't you?"

"You butcher my name," the man grumbled.

"I will butcher you!" snapped Golitsyn, his voice rising. He settled down when Slocum shook his head. More quietly, Golitsyn asked, "Where are the Fabergé treasures you stole from the tsar?"

"I personally stole nothing," said Metchnikovitch.

"Look," Slocum said, "we all know what's happened. We know you're trying to stall, hoping someone will see us. That's not going to happen." Slocum motioned for Metchnikovitch to drag first one and then the other downed revolutionary off the trail and into the undergrowth.

Outside of sight of anyone on the trail, Golitsyn demanded of Metchnikovitch, "The egg. I want the egg!"

"It's back in the fort."

"We know that," said Slocum. "Where?"

"In the safe."

Slocum pushed Golitsyn back. It wouldn't do to have the little man lose his temper. Metchnikovitch might clam up completely and require more than reasoned arguments to talk.

"Where is the safe? You tell us, you live. I don't care spit about Russian politics, but I'm going to get this booty back for the prince. I promised that much."

"If I betray the cause, you let me live? Pah!"

"If I let the prince have you, you die. Isn't it better to live to fight another day?" asked Slocum.

"You would not lie? No, I see that," said Metchnikovitch, his tone changing noticeably. "My life for the location of the egg? It seems we have made this exchange before, but under different circumstances."

"That's the deal." Golitsyn made tiny choking noises. He obviously didn't like the trade.

"On your honor? You Americans value this highly."

"I give you my word. On my honor," said Slocum.

"The safe is buried in the floor of the commandant's cabin. The southeast corner of flooring lifts up."

"Is it a combination or key safe?"

"Combination. But I do not know the combination. The commandant of Fort Ross allows us to use the safe, but only he knows how to open it."

"You lie!" flared Golitsyn, shoving Slocum aside. The instant he did that, Metchnikovitch turned and bolted into the woods like a frightened jackrabbit. Golitsyn's feet tangled with Slocum's, and they went down in a struggling heap. By the time they'd got back up, Metchnikovitch was nowhere to be seen.

"Stay here, damn your eyes!" ordered Slocum. "If he gets back to the fort, we're in hot water."

"The combination!"

"Screw the combination to the damned safe. I want out of here with all my parts." Slocum took off at an easy lope in the direction Metchnikovitch had taken. The jeweler was no better at laying a false trail than he was at being a revolutionary. Slocum soon closed the gap between them by following the broken twigs visible even in the darkness and soon heard the man blundering through the forest. Slocum picked up the pace and burst out onto the edge of one of the wheat fields. Across it he saw the redwood walls of Fort Ross rising. Metchnikovitch was a hundred yards ahead.

Slocum debated drawing and firing, then decided against it. He ran for all he was worth—and caught Metchnikovitch halfway across the field. They went down in a pile of flailing arms and legs, but Slocum knew that capture wasn't going to be easy, even though Metchnikovitch was panting heavily from his frenzied run through the forest.

"Give it up," Slocum ordered. He swung and hit the jeweler in the belly. His fist vanished into flab. Metchnikovitch didn't seem to even notice.

"Help!" Metchnikovitch cried. Slocum got one hand over the man's mouth and put the other on his celluloid collar to pull him down. It wouldn't take but one curious settler to see them in the middle of the bare wheat field.

Metchnikovitch kicked and caught Slocum in the groin. New stars filled the nighttime sky, and Slocum lost his hold for a moment. Metchnikovitch grabbed for Slocum's gun. They fought, Slocum slowly gaining the upper hand.

The single shot startled Slocum. Metchnikovitch slumped to the turned field, sightless eyes staring up at the sky.

Slocum stupidly stood and looked at his Colt. It hadn't been fired. By the time he realized that someone else had shot Metchnikovitch, Golitsyn had reached his side. The still-smoking pistol in the Russian's hand told the story.

"You fool!" said Slocum. "I had him. He could

have told us the combination and saved a world of trouble. We both know he was lying about not knowing the combination."

"You let him escape," said Golitsyn in a cold voice. "I could not risk you allowing it to happen again."

"What?" The distorted logic again surprised Slocum. "I didn't let him escape. And if I had, why would I be wrestling with him in the middle of a damned wheat field, both of us fighting over a gun?"

"Perhaps you wanted to return and kill me. Perhaps he disagreed."

"You're out of your mind," Slocum said hotly. He looked down at Metchnikovitch and heaved a sigh. "Where're the other two? Maybe they know something."

"Both are dead."

Golitsyn's bloodthirstiness extended to murdering helpless men. Slocum had been willing to think Ivan's death had been accidental—sort of. But two more? Golitsyn was as bad as any of the revolutionaries he fought against.

"Listen," Slocum said. "The shot alerted someone. Let's get back to camp and work through this." Slocum reached for his gun, but the prince's foot pressed it down into the soft dirt.

"I will keep your gun."

Slocum looked into the huge bore of Golitsyn's pistol. There wasn't much he could do but agree.

13

"The Fabergé egg is within the fort. Metchnikovitch said so." Dmitri Golitsyn had resumed his nervous pacing. The riding crop whacked repeatedly against his upper thigh, and he chewed at the tips of his mustaches. Slocum leaned back against a rock, eyes half closed, and wondered how big a callus the man had on that leg from the self-abuse. He seemed to get as much pleasure out of hitting himself as he did killing helpless men.

"We could have had the combination to the safe if the prince hadn't got antsy and shot up everyone," Slocum said.

"You, be quiet," Golitsyn snapped. "You tried to betray our cause to the Social Revolutionaries. I saw it!"

"You saw nothing," Slocum said coldly. "Those people are so disorganized they'd sell each other up the river and never know it. Metchnikovitch was going to spill his guts to me till you tried to jump him."

"This is getting us nowhere," said Juliana. "The situation is not hopeless. We still have a few hours until sunrise, when the bodies are likely to be found."

"The two won't be found unless they hunt for them. But there's no way they can miss Metchnikovitch if they go into the field," said Slocum. "Golitsyn made sure we'd fail by not even letting me hide the body."

"Do not try to force blame onto me, *asyol*," said Golitsyn. "You were making an illicit deal with Metchnikovitch."

"What did he call me?" Slocum asked Juliana.

Her face stayed calm, but Slocum knew she was nearing the end of her rope. "He called you a donkey."

"Jackass," supplied Slocum.

"Yes, that. John, is there any way of getting the egg? Any way at all?"

Slocum sighed. He wanted done with this. He was fed up with little banty rooster princes strutting around giving orders and shooting anything that moved. He was fed up with being treated like a traitor or worse. He was fed up with all the killing and misery he'd come into. All Slocum wanted out of life was to ride on north, into Oregon, and be done with the sorry lot of them. There wasn't anything under the sun that could make him change his mind.

He looked into Juliana's blue eyes and was lost.

"There's probably a way," he said. "Dangerous, especially now that our trigger-happy prince has blasted his way through four of the Social Revolutionaries."

"Dmitri," Juliana said, silencing his outcry. "We need him. Tsar Alexander needs him."

"I don't need any of you," said Slocum. "But I'm willing to give it one more try."

"For me, John?" Juliana asked so softly no one else could hear.

"I want to see what all the fuss is over," he said.

Silent communication flowed between the pair. It broke apart when Golitsyn loudly asked, "When do we return?"

"Wrong question, Golitsyn," said Slocum. "It's when do *I* return. And the answer is right now. You stay here and I'll pull your fat out of the fire for you."

"No!"

"Then no one tries it. You said yourself the safe might have to be blown. I've done a bit of that work in my day. All you've done is lead suicidal cavalry charges."

"Who told you that?" Golitsyn flared. Slocum laughed in the man's face. He hadn't known anything about the prince's military commands, but it made sense. Slocum had seen commanders like Golitsyn during the war. They thought nothing of frontal attacks that cost them more in manpower than they gained in territory, but that never seemed to matter to them. The glory of winning at any cost, no matter how trivial the triumph, or perhaps the heady thrill of leading men forward to their death meant everything to them.

Slocum had seen how Golitsyn felt about death. The jump between seeing and figuring what the man would do with his own command wasn't very big at all.

"I want my Colt back."

Slocum's green eyes stared down into the prince's hot, dark ones. Golitsyn broke away, reaching down and pulling Slocum's pistol from his belt. He thrust it forward. Slocum took it without comment.

"What are you going to do, John?"

"That's a real poser," he said. "The safe is in the fort commandant's office, or so Metchnikovitch said. When he told me that, he wasn't lying. I'm betting my life on that. It'll save a lot of looking around, but after I find it . . ." Slocum shrugged. He had no clear plan. It would all have to be played by ear.

"Good luck," Juliana said. She lifted herself up on tiptoe and kissed him. Slocum could feel the anger rising in Dmitri Golitsyn, but he ignored it. Unconcerned about the other man's feelings, he returned

Juliana's kiss with fervor, then gently pushed her away.

"Save something for when I get back—with the egg."

Slocum did a quiet sneak back down the hillside and past the same dogs that had greeted him before so noisily. He was an old friend to them by now and got into Fort Ross through the opened gate without a single warning bark being uttered. Slocum kept to deep shadows; the commandant's office still had a single lamp lit within. This bothered him. Who was guarding the safe?

He peered through the window and saw three of the Social Revolutionaries still awake and playing cards. On the far side of the room, just about where Metchnikovitch had said the safe rested under the flooring, Yerik paced back and forth.

"All these damn Russians act like caged animals," muttered Slocum. He worried over Golitsyn's easy acceptance of this little foray. Slocum had the feeling that Golitsyn had somehow set him up. But how?

And what did the prince have to gain?

Seeing Yerik acting so keyed up made Slocum wonder if the prince and the Social Revolutionaries might not be in cahoots. Then he pushed it out of his mind. He was getting as squirrely as the half-pint prince.

He had to think hard on how to get the men out of the office and himself in for long enough to check out the safe.

Slocum slipped away and scouted the rest of the enclosure. As many as fifty men slept in a barracks arrangement. Mostly bachelors, he guessed, putting in public duty—and a goodly number of them might be Social Revolutionaries. Golitsyn's plan of attacking Fort Ross seemed more and more remote in its chances of success. If Slocum didn't get the Easter egg, there'd be no way of doing it short of massacre.

He went back to the commandant's office, wiped off a dirty pane, and studied those inside. Yerik had stopped his pacing and now sat rocked back in a chair, two legs lifted and two planted squarely on the floor over the safe. The other three men had given up on their card game and were passing around a bottle of clear liquid. Slocum didn't figure it was water, from their expressions. They were all soused, but he couldn't count on that being any help.

Slocum picked up a small pebble and tossed it onto the roof. It clattered noisily in the quiet night before falling off on the far side. No one inside noticed. Slocum repeated it, with a bigger rock. This time Yerik spun around and pressed his face against the far window. He said something in Russian that the other three ignored.

None of the Social Revolutionaries took commands all that well, Slocum noticed. They didn't so much have an army as a collection of men. No one was in charge; "anarchy" came closer to describing them. He had seen how Ivan, Yerik, and Metchnikovitch all had different ideas and how, at times, each had prevailed. Without more order and a definite chain of command, the rebels worked at cross-purposes all the time. Slocum doubted Tsar Alexander had much to worry about the Social Revolutionaries overthrowing his government—the most coordinated they got was in building and throwing a bomb.

All that worked against him now. Yerik went to check on the noise and the others stayed where they were.

Slocum circled, waiting. Yerik emerged from the commandant's office, gleaming knife in hand. The instant he turned to check the far side of the office, Slocum struck. His Colt rose up and crashed down hard on the man's head. Yerik pulled his arms in to his body and slumped to the wood porch without a sound. Slocum pulled him out of sight and left him in deep shadow at one side of the structure.

"One down, three to go," he said.

Subtle maneuvers hadn't worked before, so Slocum tried a bolder frontal assault. He simply walked into the office, Colt drawn and cocked. It took the three drunk Russian revolutionaries a few seconds to understand what was happening.

"Don't," said Slocum. "You, tie up your two friends. Now!"

He had to redo the bonds on one of the men, since the job was so drunkenly done, but in less than ten minutes he had the three hog-tied and gagged and could turn his attention to the floor safe.

Slocum pulled up the boards and found the safe exactly where Metchnikovitch had said it was. The safe was securely locked. While the box was old and Slocum could open it in a few minutes given a half stick of dynamite, he had neither explosives nor time.

"Think," he said to himself. "Think and you can still get the egg. But how?"

Slocum slowly smiled as a plan formed. He said a few words to his captives, then dropped the flooring back into place. He took two short lengths of rope and hurried outside to where Yerik was beginning to stir, still groggy from the blow on the head. Slocum tied him up, making sure he could get free without too much effort.

"Thank you, Yerik," he said softly in the man's ear. "I have the Fabergé egg. That safe was easy to open."

"Swine!" grated out the Russian. "You could not open it without blowing it open."

"Don't bet on that, friend. You made it real easy for me. Real easy."

Slocum vanished into the night without a further word. He circled around and watched, waiting. Much depended on Yerik's reaction, if Slocum had under-played his hand, or if the Russian simply didn't care about losing face in front of all the others in Fort Ross.

Yerik slipped free of the ropes and rubbed his wrists. Rather than sending up a hue and cry and having those sleeping in the barracks go after Slocum, the man rushed back into the office. Slocum grinned now. he was going to pull this off after all. He had guessed right about Yerik, about the way the man thought, about not wanting to be the one responsible for letting the booty be retaken. He watched through the window as Yerik bulled his way to the safe.

"Did he open safe?" demanded Yerik.

A wild babble came from the three gagged men on the floor. Slocum had no idea what they said—he had told them he had got what he'd come for. He only hoped they had believed he had opened the safe and cleaned it out under their noses.

"Damn you all!" shrieked Yerik.

Then he did what Slocum had prayed he'd do. He hunkered down, spun the simple dial lock, and opened the safe to check to see if the treasure still rested inside.

"I don't understand," Yerik said, crouching beside the opened safe door. "All is here."

"You'll be heavier by a couple of bullets in your head if you don't move away from the safe. *Now!*" Slocum let the bite into his voice. If he hadn't, Yerik would have tried to slam and relock the safe.

"You trick me!"

"Saves a lot of wear and tear on the safe door. Nobody really wanted me blowing it open with dynamite, now would they? Might harm the jewels inside."

Yerik stood, hands balling into fists. The expression on his face was one of pure hatred. Even over the stench of spilled vodka on the table, Slocum smelled the man's sweat, the anger, the sheer animal viciousness because he had been duped.

"You're a dead man if you move even an inch," Slocum said. "Turn around." He warily forced Yerik to his knees, then tied the Russian's hands securely behind his back. Feet next, and Slocum added a gag to keep him from crying for help. Try as he might, the loudest sound Yerik could produce was a muffled grunt.

Slocum stuck the Colt back into his holster and reached into the buried safe. A large redwood box with a simple hook fastener was all that lay within. The expression on Yerik's face told him that this was what Juliana and Golitsyn and all the others had fought and killed—and died—for.

"Just want to see what the fuss is about," he said. Slocum gingerly unhooked the metal hook catch and opened the box. Inside lay the stolen treasures of Imperial Russia. For a long minute all Slocum could do was stare.

He pulled out the Siberian jade and red-gold miniature pianoforte he knew so well. It was exquisitely formed, intricately detailed, and still lovely. But it was the least of the pieces. He saw why Stephan thought he could steal it and no one would be the wiser. Compared to the other items, it was hardly noticeable.

In its own tiny box rested a flamingo like one Slocum had seen in Florida and even in some of the Georgia swamps near his homestead in Calhoun County. But this wasn't just any pink bird. This was special. The body had been fashioned from a single large pearl and the neck encased in small diamonds. Ruby eyes peered from either side of a deep coral beak. The webbed feet and legs had been made from chased green gold. Slocum's hands shook as he touched it.

"Never saw anything so lovely," he said. Yerik only grunted behind his gag.

Slocum hastily replaced the five-inch-high bird and looked at a tiny dormouse of some brown stone holding tiny gold blades of straw. The eyes were sapphire and the whiskers something Slocum took to be platinum, like he'd seen in a woman's ring. Four other animals were in the box, each detailed and each perfection in itself.

When he came to the egg, he was immensely disappointed. The white ceramic egg was smaller than a normal hen's egg and showed none of the detail the other pieces did.

"This is it?" Slocum asked, almost in disgust. "Hardly seems worth it." The expression on Yerik's face made Slocum examine the egg more closely.

A band of gold, hardly thicker than his fingernail, ran around the center of the egg. Twisting, Slocum discovered that a bayonet fitting opened the egg into two pieces.

"That's clever," he said, seeing the dull, sandblasted gold yolk, which also twisted apart to reveal a solid gold chicken sitting inside the opened egg. Each gold feather was delicately engraved, and two cabochon ruby eyes were set in the head. The comb and beak were fashioned from raw, red gold. "But any of the other..." He frowned when he noticed that the nest on which the gold chicken roosted seemed to be movable. Another gentle tug pulled the chicken off its hinged perch and revealed a tiny crown of diamonds.

Yerik struggled harder against his bonds now that Slocum had found the miniature crown.

"Let me guess," Slocum said. "This represents the Imperial Crown." He looked closely at it and, to his surprise, found another catch. He opened the crown and saw resting inside it a tiny ruby pendant too fragile for him to even dare touch.

Slocum had to stare in pure delight at the trinket.

"No wonder Ivan wanted this—no wonder Metchnikovitch did, too. A jeweler would be hard pressed to sell something this incredible, even to support a revolution." Slocum carefully repacked pendant in crown, crown in chicken, chicken in yolk, yolk in egg. The assembled white ceramic Fabergé Easter egg was hardly an inch and a half long and wasn't over two and a half inches thick.

He made sure everything was securely packed into the redwood case, which he tucked carefully under his arm.

"This is going back to its rightful owner," he told Yerik. "Tsarina Marie Feodorovna will have one fine Easter." The stricken look on Yerik's face told Slocum how the taunt hurt. The Social Revolutionaries had stolen these treasures, shipped them around the world, and intended to use them against Tsar Alexander. Now all that work, all the plans, were snuffed out in one quick theft.

Slocum left without saying another word, something unsettling nagging at the edges of his mind. He ought to have done something and hadn't. What?

Just outside Fort Ross's redwood gate, it came to him. Yerik's knife. What had happened to it? The man had come outside to investigate the noisy stone rolling down the roof. The knife had been in his hand then. Slocum had slugged him, but where did the knife go? He hadn't seen it on the porch.

Slocum shivered a little in the chill gripping the countryside. The wind off the Pacific had died, but the still, damp coldness covered him like a blanket. In only a short time the settlers would be stirring. He had to be away from Fort Ross and rejoin Juliana and Golitsyn by then. While there were only a handful of soldiers with the prince, they were trained and could hold off any attack long enough to get on the trail.

Slocum didn't really figure on there being an attack or even much pursuit. From all he'd seen, the settlers here at Slavyansk only tolerated the Social Revolutionaries. They might feed them and give them a place to stay, but there the obligation ended. The farmers would not fight for what the Social Revolutionaries believed in.

Already the sounds of cows being milked and horses stirring sounded across the meadowland. Slocum gripped the redwood box holding the Fabergé jewels and quickened his pace.

He had reached the base of the hill leading up to Golitsyn's camp when it hit him.

"Yerik's knife. He must still have it!"

Even as the thought came to him, he heard the soft

crunch of thin ice cracking under boots. Slocum swung around, hand going for his pistol. Yerik slashed savagely with the knife, opening a narrow gash along Slocum's right arm.

The redwood box tumbled to the ground.

"You will die for this," Yerik said.

"Ivan's dead," said Slocum, moving to be able to pull his pistol with his left hand. His right refused to close; he didn't think Yerik had done any serious damage, but he couldn't be certain. Whatever had happened because of the cut, the nerves had been momentarily deadened, making his right hand useless. "So's Metchnikovitch."

"When I saw you, I knew that to be true. They died for cause! Now you die, too!"

Yerik came in fast, low, and deadly. The tip of the thin-bladed flensing knife that had done service on seals now sought to gut Slocum. He failed to get his gun out. Instead, he batted aside the tip of the blade and tried to grab Yerik's wrist.

They both went down in a pile, kicking and futilely striking at one another. Slocum gasped when another gash opened along his ribs. He rolled away and got to his feet, only to find Yerik still after him.

"Ivan would not let me kill you in warehouse. I was right. You have meddled too much. This gives me pleasure now."

Slocum avoided the knife thrust and danced away. Clumsily he reached around and got the butt of his pistol with his left hand. His right still refused to close properly. Yerik saw that he would be at a disadvantage allowing Slocum to get his pistol out. He closed in a rush, arms circling Slocum's body.

Slocum grunted as he felt powerful arms crushing

him in a bear hug. Even worse, the tip of the knife was beginning to drive into his back.

He pulled the trigger on his Colt, even though it wasn't aimed anywhere useful. The explosion startled Yerik enough that he relaxed his grip. Bloodied, hurting, Slocum kicked backward and got away.

Like a glacier, cold, implacable, Yerik kept coming.

Slocum had his Colt out and in his left hand now.

Awkwardly, he pulled the trigger. The heavy .44 slug went wide and to the left, not even coming close to Yerik.

The Russian landed on Slocum with both knees pressing him into the turf. One knee held his gun hand flat to the ground. The other drove the wind from his lungs. Weakly thrashing, Slocum used his right hand more as a club than a fist. He batted away another knife thrust aimed for his heart.

But consciousness fled. He couldn't breathe. His right hand was numb, and his left was pinned.

Knowing this might be the last effort he could— or would—make, Slocum heaved, turned to the left, and used his legs to give him added leverage. Yerik toppled to one side, but cat agile, didn't fall hard enough to lose his balance.

Slocum's right hand twitched spastically, but he managed to clamp it weakly on a sharp rock. He swung with it and cut Yerik's face just under the eye. As the Russian winced, Slocum got completely out from under, his left hand again finding his Colt.

Slocum turned, saw Yerik readying for another attack, and pulled the trigger. This gunshot was muffled. Yerik's body pressed fully against the muzzle as the heavy slug ripped through his guts. The Russian raised his knife, paused, then fell backward, stiff as a board. The knife clattered downhill until it lay against a dark rock.

Slocum closed his eyes and sucked in huge drafts of air until he felt steady again. The knife cuts were bleeding but not too badly. They'd scab over soon enough. He massaged his right wrist, got some feeling back into it, and then reholstered his pistol. Slocum picked up the redwood box holding the Fabergé treasures.

Another man has died because of you, you son of a bitch, he thought about the Russian tsar. *I hope you're satisfied.*

Slocum took only two steps up the hill when a sixth sense warned him of another presence. He started to draw his Colt when a voice he knew only too well told him, "That will not be necessary, Slocum."

Prince Golitsyn rose from the shelter of a boulder and stepped forward. He had witnessed the entire fight with Yerik and hadn't bothered to come to Slocum's aid.

It took all the will power John Slocum possessed not to simply pull the trigger one more time. This would have been one death he would have enjoyed.

14

Slocum waited for the blast to shatter his spine. It never came. They reentered the tiny camp and Juliana rose up from her bedroll, eyes dancing and alive.

"Did you . . . ?" she asked.

Slocum held up the redwood box for all to see. Golitsyn took it from him and set it down by a small campfire and carefully went through the valuable contents. Juliana crowded close behind Golitsyn, oohs and ahs of excitement escaping her lips as she saw first one Fabergé item and then another. Both countess and prince took their time examining the Easter egg.

Slocum didn't blame them, but he maintained an aloofness. He had seen the baubles and didn't need a second look. He thought this made him just a little better than Golitsyn. Why that ought to matter to him, Slocum didn't rightly know.

"Oh, John, I knew you could do it!" Juliana threw her arms around his neck, pulled his face down, and soundly kissed him. This wasn't just a thank-you kiss either. It carried the full message of her sexuality with it. She wanted him.

And Slocum had to admit he wanted her, too.

He had been through a hell of a lot and felt he deserved something. There wouldn't be any money coming his way. At least no more'n he had already got. The thick wad of bills he had taken off Shanghai

Kelly still rode high in his shirt pocket. That was going to get him all the way north to Oregon and set him up in business. For the spring, and maybe longer, depending on how the horse trade was.

While he thought the Fabergé jewelry was the finest he'd ever seen, Slocum had no use for it. Things weren't supposed to be just looked at. They had to be useful, too.

Juliana Rumyantsova was lovely to look at, but she was also an intelligent woman, warm and good in bed and all any man could ask for. Simply looking at her would be a damnfool waste.

"John," she started, her slender hand running lightly down the front of his shirt, then finding a way to sneak between the buttons and onto bare skin.

"We ride. Now," Slocum said. "Most of the ones I picked out as leaders of the Social Revolutionaries are dead. I killed Yerik down the hill. Ivan's already dead and so is Metchnikovitch. But they don't seem to be too organized. They might have a dozen others willing to step in and get a party up after us."

"We ride," Juliana agreed. She motioned to the Russian soldiers. They began saddling up. "But we can't ride forever," she said so that only Slocum overheard. "And then . . . " Juliana's fingers worked lower and found the bulge in his trousers. She squeezed down, and he started to respond to that light touch.

"Then," he promised.

He felt so stiff he almost busted, and getting onto a horse was close to being torture. But his hard-on went away as they cut toward the ocean and followed the line of trees on a different path leading toward San Francisco.

Juliana fell back a ways when the trail narrowed and began twisting in and out of the redwoods. Slocum used the opportunity to spur his horse forward and draw even with Golitsyn.

"Got something to ask you, Prince," he said.

The man's mustaches twitched slightly. Other than this, there was no sign he had even heard Slocum.

"You watched while Yerik came after me with the knife. You saw my hand was all banged up and I was well-nigh helpless. How come you didn't help me?"

"Slocum, really," said the prince with a superior air. "You were doing all right by yourself. If I had fired, I might have struck you rather than Yerik."

"Wouldn't have bothered you much, would it? Bet you'd've even liked to use a second bullet."

Golitsyn smiled, and it wasn't a pleasant sight. Slocum let the Russian nobleman ride on ahead with the main body of the soldiers. He reined in until Juliana was again at his side.

"He tried to get me killed," said Slocum. "I know he never much liked me, but this is different. Yerik might have killed me, and then Golitsyn would have shot down Yerik and taken the Fabergé jewelry."

"Dmitri's not such a bad sort," Juliana said, defending him. "I'm sure he didn't arrive in time to help you. There's no reason for him to want to see you dead, John. Believe me. All we wanted was to recover the Easter egg for the tsar."

"Too many people died for that gaud," he said.

"No one will know that," Juliana said, almost sorrowfully. "I wish we could reward you with a title, or at least a medal, but we cannot. It is beyond any of our powers to acknowledge your help in this touchy political matter."

Slocum nodded. He knew why. Tsar Alexander dared not let the public know that his palace security had been breached and valuable property stolen. That would only encourage the Social Revolutionaries into trying again. They would know that some of their number had died, and that would be good enough. No one—Slocum included—doubted that the rebels already planned some other mad scheme. It took more than death to deter a fanatic.

"But there can be other types of reward. Ones that are not official but which might be more . . . enjoyable." Juliana turned slightly in her saddle. The top three buttons of her blouse had come unfastened. Soft swells of white breast pressed up and threatened to spill out at any moment.

Slocum wanted to be there when they did.

"We'll ride most of the day," he said. Slocum craned his neck to peer ahead along the trail. "That ought to get us far enough away from Fort Ross to keep anyone from following."

"With Metchnikovitch and Yerik and Ivan all gone, they will not quickly find a new leader. They are nihilists, intent only on disrupting. Their planners are eliminated. They preach reform but have no clear plan for achieving it. No, John, they will not follow now that their top men are dead."

The rest of the day went by as if it had been dipped in molasses. Slocum knew they were making good time along this winding seacoast trail, even though Golitsyn had insisted they take a longer route back to San Francisco. Slocum hadn't protested. An extra few nights on the trail with Juliana might be just the thing for getting over the feeling that he had been used—and badly.

The redwood forest produced a heady scent; the burning wood and salt tang from the ocean added to it. Their simple trail supper was over quickly. Golitsyn ordered out most of the Russian soldiers and posted them at odd places around the campsite. Slocum started to ask why the prince had chosen such inaccessible sentry points, then found other, more enjoyable questions to ask.

"Where's a spot away from the others?" he asked Juliana.

"A countess is due some privacy," she said. "I have my bedroll laid out over there." She pointed to a secluded spot hidden under a rocky outjutting.

"That's not the only thing that's going to get laid out tonight," Slocum said, grinning.

"Americans are long on promise but short on delivery. Are you typical?" she asked, teasing.

"You decide," he said, unfastening his gunbelt and lowering his trousers. His cock poked out, eager and hard.

"No," Juliana said softly. "You are not like most. You are long, so very, wonderfully long!"

Cold air gusted around the rocks, through the tall redwoods, and past Slocum's erection. He shivered and felt himself starting to turn flaccid. Juliana moved closer, her hand gripping down on him. The gentle warmth kept him hard. Then her mouth began doing things, touching and kissing and sucking and exciting him till there was no longer any worry about him turning limp.

They sank down to the softness of the bed Juliana had prepared. Beneath her blanket she had placed pine needles and other mulch to cushion their bodies as they passionately wrestled.

The simple act of lying down crushed pine needles and released a fragrance that met and merged with the sexy musk odor of the aroused woman. Slocum reached down and put his hands on either side of her head. Gently he pried her away from her erotic post, lifted her up, and kissed her full on her lush, red lips.

"Oh, John, I've waited so long for this. We've been through so much!"

"It's past now. Your tsarina will get her Easter present."

"And you'll get yours early," Juliana said, her tongue flicking out and lightly touching his earlobe. *"We'll* get ours!"

Her hot breath aroused Slocum even more. Agile fingers found buttons and fasteners. Juliana laid back and arched up so that he could strip her of the useless clothing. Then it was Juliana's turn to do the same for him. Icy winds whipped through the forest; the blanket over them felt good.

But not as good as the warmth of naked flesh against equally naked flesh.

They kissed and touched, Slocum's hands moving from the soft cheeks to Juliana's slender neck—and lower. She sighed in rapture when he cupped her breasts, holding those firm mounds and slowly twisting from one side to another. When he sucked on an already hard nipple, Juliana gasped, arched her back, and thrust her chest forward.

"More, John my darling, I want more."

He gave it to her.

They explored each other's body with gentle slowness, until their desires built to the point where they could barely control themselves. More animalistic passions ruled them then. Their kisses became harder, more insistent. Fingernails raked at Slocum's broad back, urging him to do more.

His own hands worked along the countess's slightly domed belly, slowed, then touched the crinkly mass of fleecy down between her legs. Juliana sobbed with need now.

He gently spread her legs wider and found the moist patch waiting for him.

"Hurry, John darling, do it. Oh, yes, do it, do it now!" the woman gasped out. Her words melted one into another. Her desires knew no bounds. She was lost in a world of passion only one thing could sate.

Slocum gave it to her.

He rolled between those wantonly parted legs and moved quickly. He felt as if he would bust at any instant. He found the damp entryway, then slowly inserted himself until he was lost in her humid interior. The woman's strong muscles clamped down on him. Slocum pulled back slightly, a lewd sucking noise the result.

Neither could restrain their rampaging needs any longer. Slocum didn't even try. He began moving faster and faster, the friction of his manhood against Juliana's interior burning them both. She gasped and lifted her behind off the ground. Her fingers clutched at his back, his upper arms. Eyes closed, she tossed her head from side to side, emitting tiny animal moans of pure ecstasy.

They both soared over the brink of total pleasure at the same time. Their bodies ground together in a carnal mix that lasted for an eternity—and then ended.

Arms cradling Juliana, Slocum lay exhausted. His passion had momentarily been sated, but he still felt the tensions in his belly. He would be ready for another bout soon. He buried his face in Juliana's fresh-scented hair and thought he could spend the rest of his life just like this.

He told her so.

"I wish that was possible, John," she said, her voice dreamy.

He started to ask her why it wasn't when a curious

gurgling noise caused him to sit bolt upright.

"John, what's wrong?"

He motioned Juliana to silence even as he hastily dressed. Slocum reloaded his Colt and shoved it back into its holster.

"John?"

"Did you hear that sound?" he asked, his eyes darting from left to right and back, scanning the forest for any sign of movement. He saw nothing.

"I guess so. Sounded like a brook."

"Could have been, but there's no running water nearby. And that's not an ocean sound. Not like any I've ever heard. Might have been a man getting his throat cut."

"What? John, no, you're imagining things." Juliana began to dress, too.

"I didn't like the way Golitsyn placed the sentries. Too far apart. Too vulnerable. Not good military planning. If any of the Social Revolutionaries from Fort Ross trailed us, they could be working their way down into camp right now."

Juliana started to rise. He quietly pushed her back down and motioned for her to stay under cover.

Slocum crouched down and began slowly circling the camp. He didn't like the silence greeting him. He widened the circle and found where a few of the Russian officers had spread their bedrolls. All had been knifed in their sleep. Grimly he worked his way to the perimeter of the camp where Golitsyn had stationed the guards.

One after another he found dead, all knifed in the back. And the one guard who had his throat slit had been the one whose gurgling cries he had overheard. If there hadn't been a lull in the wind blowing off the ocean, his death cry would have gone undetected.

"What's wrong?" came an all too familiar voice.

"Golitsyn," said Slocum. He had never thought he'd be relieved to see the small prince. "Someone's killed the guards. All of them."

"Impossible. These were handpicked men. All elite."

"An Indian could have done it," said Slocum. "Or..." He turned to face the prince and saw the large-caliber pistol in his hand. "Or someone they didn't suspect."

The last thing Slocum saw was Golitsyn's body wracked with mocking laughter. The last thing he heard was the cannon's roar as the pistol discharged. He jerked about under the bullet's impact and lay face down on the forest floor.

Slocum wasn't sure how long he had been lying there before he felt soft fingers stroking over his head. He winced, the pain slamming into him like a hammer blow.

"Don't," came the distant command. "I want to stop the bleeding."

"Juliana?"

"You're going to be all right. Th—the guards are all dead." Only the faint quaver in her voice betrayed emotion. Slocum worked to get his eyes open. Juliana, as lovely as ever, was tending to him. He hadn't realized it, but she had rolled him over and cradled his head in her lap. She pressed down firmly on the bandage she held and closed the wound in his scalp.

"Where's Golitsyn?"

"I don't know," she said. "Hold this in place while I get something more to bind it." She came back a few minutes later with a roll of bandages. "One of the nice things about traveling with military men.

They always carry an ample supply of bandages. We learned those bitter lessons in the Crimea." She fastened the bandage in place.

Slocum didn't feel any better, but the bleeding had stopped. His entire body aching, he sat up. The dizziness passed quickly, and he looked about.

"Golitsyn killed the guards," he said. "Why?"

"He would have killed me, too," Juliana said. "He took the Fabergé pieces. A prince in the Imperial Guard and he stole Tsar Alexander's property! He betrayed his oath!"

"Did he think I was dead?"

"I am sure he did. And he couldn't find me. When I heard the gunshot, I hid. I actually thought the Social Revolutionaries had caught up with us again. Dmitri searched and called out my name, but I saw the smoking gun in his hand. When you didn't return, I . . . I caught on to what happened." Again emotion threatened to take control. Juliana fought it back.

"Good thing," said Slocum. "My gun! The little son of a bitch took my gun!"

"He stripped all the men. Guns, valuables. Just like a common road agent, he stole everything of value."

Slocum touched the shirt pocket where he had carried his poke. All the greenbacks were gone, too.

"Golitsyn will regret this," said Slocum in a stony voice. "If I have to use my bare hands, he'll regret this."

Juliana silently reached into a pocket and pulled out the Remington .41 derringer. "I took this from you, back in San Francisco. You remember?"

"I remember what happened before you stole it and the jade pianoforte," said Slocum. "But the shot to the head seems to have made me forget seeing you traipsing down the street with my clothes."

Juliana kissed him.

"Enough of that," he said. "How long was I unconscious?" He took the derringer from her and checked it. She hadn't reloaded it after shooting the thief who had tried to steal the jade Fabergé miniature. He had only one shot to get Golitsyn.

"Not long. But Dmitri took all the horses, too. We're on foot."

Slocum tried to remember the lay of the land, where Golitsyn was most likely to go.

"We've got to hurry. The trail winds around and then comes back. If we go straight down the cliff facing the ocean we might be able to stop him."

"Why do you think he'll go toward the Pacific?"

"Easier traveling both north and south. From here all he can do is go east into the Sierras. Nothing much for a man like him there. I'm betting on him wanting to return to San Francisco, but not wasting any more time on doing it."

Slocum took the countess's hand and pulled her along behind. He staggered a bit at the start but grew stronger. Determination fed him and kept him going, even to the tall cliff overlooking the ocean.

"He has to wind his way down the trail way over there and then come back in this direction. We don't have to worry about horses. We go straight down."

Juliana swallowed, then nodded. Slocum doubted that the woman trusted herself to speak. They started the descent, cutting their hands, scraping their knees, and almost plunging to their death several times. But they arrived on the sandy beach, tired and aching in every muscle.

They also arrived in time to see Golitsyn leading a string of horses down a twisting path some distance away.

"You were right, John," Juliana said. "We got down here before him. But what do we do now? We can't stop him. He has all the guns and the horses."

Slocum touched the derringer. All it would take was one shot.

They ran through the wet sand, the effort pulling away at their stamina with every step. But as Juliana fell behind, Slocum kept moving. He had figured out the spot where Golitsyn would reach the sandy shoreline. From there he could go either north or south with ease—Slocum guessed south toward San Francisco rather than north past Fort Ross.

As he ran, Slocum scooped up a long piece of driftwood. The rotted exterior hid a more solid core. He positioned himself behind a rock, waiting. He had regained his breath by the time he heard the gentle crunching of horses' hooves on the sand. He circled the large rock, then climbed atop it as Golitsyn rode past.

Some slight noise betrayed Slocum. The prince spun in the saddle just as Slocum got to the top of the boulder and started his swing. Golitsyn ducked, but the driftwood struck him high on the shoulder and unseated him. Slocum dived over the horse and landed hard on the prince.

Frustration, rage, the need for revenge all burned bright in Slocum. He put every ounce of power he could muster into the blow that landed squarely on Golitsyn's pointed chin. He felt the man's head snap back and the life flee his body. Dmitri Golitsyn sprawled, arms outstretched, on the sand.

Panting from the exertion, Slocum stood up and wiped the sweat off his forehead. His hand came away caked with sand.

"John, John! Are you all right?" Juliana ran up and stopped, staring down at Golitsyn.

"Just fine—now."

He took her in his arms, and, after the wracking sobs had passed, he kissed her.

"It's all right now. Just—"

"Just nothing," came shaky words. Golitsyn sat up, his pistol in his hand. "I thought I had finished you, Slocum. You continually surprise me. If I didn't know you for the barbarian you are, I'd think you were Russian."

"Don't talk about barbarians, Golitsyn," said Slocum, cursing his own stupidity. He should have murdered the bastard when he had the chance, but Juliana had distracted him. It might be the last mistake he'd ever make. "I'm not the one who killed a dozen of his own men in cold blood. Did you enjoy it?"

"Not really. They were fine men, brave men. But they lacked vision. None would see what I do."

"And what's that, Dmitri?" asked Juliana. Slocum pushed her to one side. If the shooting started, he didn't want her being the first hit. He swallowed hard—it wasn't *if* the shooting started but *when*.

Dmitri Golitsyn would not let either of them live this time.

"I have no love for the tsar. And lovely Juliana, you fail to see the turmoil brewing in Russia. The Social Revolutionaries are clowns, buffoons, but others will come along who are not. Russia cannot survive. One day the tsar will be overthrown and the peasants will try to rule." Golitsyn spat. "There is no place for one such as I in a country ruled by serfs."

"You figure on living it up by selling the egg and the other items, is that it?" asked Slocum.

"There are civilized countries in Europe that will welcome me with open arms," Golitsyn said. "Carl Fabergé's trinkets will keep me in style for some time."

"Run, Juliana!" Slocum cried, shoving the woman hard to the right. She was off balance and fell onto her face, but Golitsyn reacted as Slocum had hoped. Instinctively the man's revolver followed the woman's path. The gun exploded, its heavy bullet passing through the space Juliana would have occupied had she actually been running. As it was, the slug went over her head, missing her by scant inches.

Slocum had the double derringer out and aimed even as Golitsyn realized his mistake. He had followed the wrong person. He should have shot at Slocum, not the countess.

John Slocum had made too many mistakes on the side of decency. He didn't make a mistake now. His finger came back smoothly on the trigger. The .41-caliber bullet found its target between Golitsyn's eyes.

The Russian prince jerked back, mustaches twitching, and lay dead on the shore, the thin trickle of blood from the head wound sucked up by the sandy beach.

15

Slocum awoke with luscious, soft, buttery sunshine in his face. He mumbled to himself and rolled over in the soft bed and felt the warm hip next to him.

"You are up earlier today," said Juliana, her hand resting on his naked flank. She scooted closer. The pair of them fit together well, Slocum thought. Maybe too well.

The trip back to San Francisco with the Fabergé treasures had been uneventful, unless you called his damn near passing out most of the time nothing. The head wound he'd got from Golitsyn, the cuts from Yerik, and the general lack of sleep had finally caught up with him. But he hadn't given in to the weakness and had escorted Juliana back safely. For two days after returning to Juliana's small house on the slope of Russian Hill he had felt like shit. For another two he dozed but was all right.

For the past week Slocum had never felt better— and a good part of that was because of Juliana's loving care.

And her loving.

"Have good reason to," he said, reaching for her. They kissed, and soon the kiss turned into more, much more. They made love, the sun shining on their naked, passionately engaged bodies. Afterward they both dozed off.

When Slocum again awoke it was past noon and the sun had moved across the room. Clouds were building up in the northern sky, and he knew that another storm would soon enough sock in San Francisco with rain and fog and other blustery winter weather.

But it wouldn't be soon enough.

The Fabergé egg had to be returned to Tsar Alexander in time to present to his wife as an Easter gift. The distance between San Francisco and St. Petersburg was vast, almost more than Slocum could imagine. The Pacific had to be crossed, then the entire continent of Asia. Two months of hard travel was probably cutting it fine. Juliana Rumyantsova had been waiting for the next steamer heading for the Russian port of Archangel. It had been almost ten days from the time they had arrived back in San Francisco till now.

The *Papootnee Veter*—the *Fair Wind*—left on the evening tide. Juliana had to be on that ship or she'd miss any chance she had of reaching St. Petersburg in time.

Slocum didn't want her to go, and he dreaded the suggestion Juliana was sure to make concerning her departure.

From the kitchen came sounds of food being prepared. He couldn't get over how good a cook Juliana was for someone who, by her own words, had lived all her life with servants doing the menial work. He guessed she had spent more than a little time in Paris learning her superb culinary skills. Once she had hinted at an illicit affair with a commoner, a French chef. Slocum didn't pursue that. It was none of his business. If that Frenchman had taught her how to cook, he'd done a damn fine job.

Slocum didn't know if he enjoyed eating the food as much as Juliana did fixing it.

"Come and get it or I'll throw it to the hogs," Juliana called.

Slocum rose and dressed slowly. He had nothing to be sad about, yet he was. The man knew the inevitable was coming, and he'd just as soon avoid it.

"Here you go," Juliana said cheerfully, putting a plate of eggs in front of him. But calling it "a plate of eggs" did it an injustice. She had put in things Slocum couldn't begin to identify. That didn't stop him from wolfing down the food.

"Not so fast, John," she said. "There's plenty of time."

Even as she said it, Juliana knew that wasn't true.

"The ship leaves in less than six hours," Slocum said. "I'll miss you."

Her bright blue eyes welled up with tears. Juliana reached out, took one of his hands, and held it tightly. "It doesn't have to be that way, John. We both know this. You have nothing pulling you north. Horses? The finest horses in the world are on the Ukrainian steppes. I can buy you the finest of Polish Arabians. We can go to England. Horses are nothing, John."

He didn't answer immediately. Horses weren't the root of it, and they both knew it.

"I won't go with you, Juliana," he said. "Russia's not my country. I wouldn't fit in with the likes of Golitsyn."

"He . . . he is not typical," she said.

"No, but I reckon the tsar's two brothers—Vladimir and Alexis, you said—I reckon they are. Wastrels getting drunk every night in that Cubat's Restaurant. Screwing their way across Europe. They're grand dukes, just a step away from the throne. Those are the people I'd be socializing with?" He shook his head and went back to the eggs. Somehow they tasted like ashes in his mouth now.

"The tsar will be grateful for the return of the egg," she said. "There would be vast rewards. Not public ones, but land, money, perhaps even a title."

"Count Slocum?" he asked. He rolled the title around and it fell off the tip of his tongue, just the way a drop of mercury refused to do more than roll around the edge of a penny.

"It doesn't sound quite right, does it?" Juliana said. "But I'll be there. We can be together."

He shook his head again, dropping his fork onto the plate with a clatter. "It'd never work out right for us, Juliana. I wish to hell it would, but it can't."

"We can try!"

"You can, maybe. I can't."

"The horses?"

"Not that. Not exactly. What you're offering me is prison. Dress balls. People thinking they're better than other folks because they have fancy-ass titles. Riding around in carriages. Living in castles. For me, that's worse than Yuma Prison."

"Is it?" She had a way of making all his arguments sound wrong. But deep down inside Slocum knew he was right. How could he explain to a countess the feel of riding alone through the Sierra Madres during spring thaw, seeing the wildflowers poking up, listening to streams bursting with crystal clear, pure water, seeing the brightly plumed birds going through their mating rituals, singing and flying free in the air?

Freedom. He wouldn't have it in Russia, not like Juliana had. He didn't speak the language, although she claimed French was spoken in the court. That made it even worse. He didn't speak *either* of the languages. Even if they left for England, as Juliana had suggested, it wasn't the kind of place he'd be comfortable in. He'd never feel he could just saddle up and ride off to see what was under that rainbow arching over the horizon or what new devilment he could get into just by weathering a Texas dust storm or Blue Norther coming across the Plains. How could he trade living by his wits for a life of servants putting and doing for him?

John Slocum couldn't.

Juliana read the answer on his face. Her hands shook, and she tried to hide the emotions rising within her. She failed. The tears that had been held back now started rolling down her cheeks. She dabbed at them, but more formed.

"There's no need to cry," he told her. "You're going home."

"Yes," she said.

"I'm already home. It won't be the same without you, but we're both better off in worlds we know. You belong in a ball gown decked out with pearls and maybe even one of the flashy Fabergé brooches you told me about. You belong to society, strutting around with kings and emperors. I don't."

"You'll always be my prince," she said softly. He had no words for that. None were needed.

The *Fair Wind* hooted its foghorn to signal that all the passengers should be aboard. Juliana stood beside Slocum on the dock, the redwood box containing the Fabergé egg and other items under her arm. She did not trust it to even the purser's safe.

"There's still time, John. I can arrange it," she said.

He looked down into her blue eyes.

"Oregon's a big country," he said. "You might come up with me. There's plenty of folks on the ship who could see that the package gets back on time."

"I can't," she said.

"I can't either, Juliana."

They kissed, almost chastely. Juliana Rumyantsova stepped back and smiled weakly, then hurried up the gangplank without saying another word to him.

Slocum watched as the *Fair Wind* got up steam, blew its horn again, and pulled away from the pier. Juliana stood on deck, her luxurious cape draped around her shoulders. She waved.

The last Slocum saw of the countess she was vanishing into the thick San Francisco fog. He stood watching the gray bank of mist long after the ship was gone. He turned and mounted his horse, spurring toward the north. He was a week or two later than he'd planned, but Oregon was still there. With luck he'd reach it soon enough.

With memories.